Mitch's Dream

- a surfer's story -

Novels by Peter Randolph Keim

TA Buck Western Sagas
Reckoning on Blood River
Erastus: Long Trail til Sundown
Renegade Guns of Pomo Point
Stoney Bray: Last Sheriff in Cripple Creek

Kate Kingshott Western Novels
Goose Lake Rustlers
Black Widow Sheriff

Jesse Crater Mysteries
Deep Threat: Murphys Gold
Hidden Threat: Ghost Boy
Sudden Threat: Reunion
Buried Threat: Dead on the Vine
Sacred Threat: Deadly Vow of Trust
Hollow Threat: Curse of the Ghost Walk

Seraphim Fantasy Novels
Eli's Rock
Charley's Ride
Reggie's Plan B
Mitch's Dream

Sci-fi Fantasy
Soddermast

Mitch's Dream

- a surfer's story -

by

Peter Randolph Keim

KeimRanchBooks

This is a work of fiction. Names, characters, characters depicted on the cover artwork, places and incidents, are products of the author's imagination or are used fictitiously and are not to be construed as real. Any resemblance to actual events, locales, organizations, or persons living or dead, is entirely coincidental.

Copyright 2012, Mount Vernon, WA

First Printing: 2012

Cover design/illustration: P. Randolph Keim
Editor: Gini Holcomb

Printed in the United States of America.

For all who search for their own Bombora.
And for those of us blessed to find it.

"Out of the water I am nothing.
In the water the rest of the world means nothing."
Anonymous

One

"Mitch."

"BeeBee."

"You taking flippers this trip?" She never missed a chance to kid him about his getting too old for serious surfing.

"Flippers?" He groused. "I'm a shreddin' surfer dude. Not a scuba geek. 'Sides, the boys don't need 'em anymore, and my feet are plenty big enough."

"You know what they say about a guy with big feet, don't you?" Sandy kidded.

"He has a big heart?" Mitch replied.

"Well, yeah, there's that."

"His big smile?" Mitch grinned.

"Best you quit while you're ahead, *Shreddin' Surfer Dude.*" She laughed, turned back to the kitchen counter. "You still want the peanut butter and banana sandwich?"

"Surfer Dude says *yes*. Thank you."

Mitch sat at the small kitchen table pawing through his cash for the trip. He and his four best friends were meeting at Mitch and Sandy's house before leaving for Ejido Chapala, south of Ensenada, Baja. They risked life and limb on Highway 1 every year as soon as they could clear their collective summer calenders. This year, it took well into summer before they could get twenty days free of societal encumbrances for the annual trip. Three of the men were teachers, one a lawyer, the other owned a coffee shop.

Out front of Mitch and Sandy's modest, stucco home, Dog finally pulled up in his '66, blue, VW bus. As always, his bus loaded with surfboards. One empty seat up front for Mitch. Already parked across the street, Stinger, Pounder and Mondo jumped out of Stringer's '67, velvet green and white VW bus. *Newer*, he'd tease Dog.

"They're here, Mitch," Sandy said from the kitchen sink. "And your sandwich is ready."

He was a kid when it came to these four guys.

Mitch ran, no, *danced*, from the kitchen. Out the front door where the five of them did a variety of handshakes and gyrations not fit for children under thirteen.

"*Dog!*" Mitch barked. "I thought your court case would last forever."

"Might have. Paid the defendant to plead guilty." Dog said.

The others stopped their greeting. "You paid him?"

"Yep."

"Was he guilty?"

"Hell, no!" Laughed Dog. "But when I gotta surf, *I gotta surf.*"

Uncontrolled laughter.

Mitch slid his surfboard and small bag of gear into Dog's bus with the other boards and small bags. After a hug and kiss with Sandy, he piled into the co-pilot seat with Dog. Mondo and Pounder flipped a coin for the co-pilot seat in Stringer's bus, then jumped in. Mitch ran back for a second hug with Sandy. Could never get enough.

"*Mitch!*" Howled Stringer. "C'mon! Leave BeeBee alone. Let's roll."

Another round of kisses. He held Sandy for a long time before letting go. "You be okay?" Mitch asked.

"Sure. Miss the snot outta you as always, but I'll be fine." She said. She loved his warm, hazel eyes. Like his mouth, they had an intrinsic smile, even when sad. "You looking forward to seeing the boys?"

"Yep."

"I can only imagine Felipe's excitement knowing you are on the way." She said.

"Paco said he hasn't slept for two days."

"Or surfed?" Sandy said.

Mitch laughed. "Not supposed to, but you can never tell with Felipe."

She kissed him one more time. "I love you, Beach Bum."

"You're such a honey. I love you."

Mitch closed the door to the bus. Stringer pulled away in his bus just ahead of them. Mitch slid the window open. "See you in three weeks."

She waved. Then, "Can I have your peanut butter and banana sandwich?"

He laughed. "Save it til I get back."

"*Mitch!*"

He laughed.

Dog's bus coughed. He slammed the gas peddle to the floor. And as gnarly as a a sailboat with no wind, the forty horsepower engine pushed the bus into the street.

It wasn't pretty, but it was very cool.

Two

As with every year, the five surfing compadres drove to Ensenada for the first night. Then on down Highway 1 to Lazaro Cardenas. They spent that night in a small hotel, and then the next day stocked up on all the supplies they'd need for their stay in Ejido Chapala.

They usually slipped out of Lazaro Cardenas before first light so as not to be seen by other surfers on the hunt for bigger and better waves.

It was purely by chance the men had found the small beach off the Baja coast where few surfed. It was far out of the way off the beaten path. Were it not for Stringer's bus getting stuck in soft sand, the men would have never met Paco. A man with a tow truck.

Paco was a local and the father of Manuel, Manny, a boy of only eight when they first met the five surfers from San Diego. Manny was a Down syndrome kid who could smile the feathers off a seagull. Paco, his father, was a single dad who, had a penchant for surfing, but had never surfed.

In the hush of the dunes and cool ocean breeze that night fifteen years ago, whispers in the dark were shared between the tow truck driver and five eager surfers. After swearing to keep the secret, Paco took the men to his private shore. The breakers that slipped around an unnamed island were the best they'd ever seen. The Pacific Ocean pushed her waters straight at the island where they split to either side then converged again behind towards the beach. The resultant waves were consistently shoulder high with an occasional larger one. Mitch and his friends preferred a full day of good waves versus waiting for a few good ones. And at their ages, shoulder high was a good breaker to surf.

Paco's secret beach gave them that.

And much more. It gave the men a handful of mentally *challenged* boys.

Manny, as the Americans, called him was the first to connect with the charismatic men. Immediately followed by Felipe, both just eight years old then now twenty-three. Other boys, some quite engaging, emerged out of the dunes. Unattended by siblings or adults.

And still others arrived at the beach surrounded by grateful family who sat on the beach all day to watch the Americans work with their *special* boys.

The men always brought along a couple extra boards, usually long boards. They would push the youngsters out, sometimes three to a board. They were too young to surf, but loved the ride. With each passing year, the boys grew stronger and the men offered them more. Each year they brought another extra surf board until they had at least eight extras. They left them there year round, under lock and key with Paco and strict instructions to never let the boys take them out on their own.

After fourteen years of annual visits, all the boys were reasonably good surfers. Especially Felipe and Raul. Good athletes. Strong, smart and fearless.

This would be the fifteenth year the men slithered into Ejido Chapala unnoticed by the other surfers perusing the surf from Highway 1 for the ideal waves. Now, all in their sixties, most had decided this might be their last trip. But no one wanted to discuss it at length.

The hot days rushed by. The surfing was, as usual, terrific. The boys were much improved, especially Felipe and Raul. Even Manny was showing signs of some serious moves on his board.

The days and nights slipped by. With only three days left, Felipe began his annual pestering for Mitch to take him to the unnamed island they all referred to as No-Name Island.

"Too tired, Felipe." Mitch would plead.

"Chicken!" Was the boy's response. Felipe was now twenty-three. Big and strong. Could surf with the best of them. He was already far better than Mitch. Even better then Pounder, considered the best of the five men.

"Not chicken." Mitch said.

"Lazy."

"Maybe."

"Old and lazy." Felipe kidded.

"Hey, Dude, who you callin' old?"

Paco, sitting with his son, Manny, and another Down syndrome boy, Raul, laughed. His belly shook under his stained t-shirt. Raul didn't understand, but laughed because his Paco did.

"Felipe," Mitch said, "Your mother would skin me if I took you out to No-Name Island, and you know it."

"Mother not here."

"Hey! Didn't I teach you better than that?"

"Yes." Felipe said, his shoulders sagged in defeat. "Mitch is right."

Mitch turned to face Felipe. "It's not about *who* is right, Felipe, but *what* is right. We both know your mother's wishes are for you to never go to the island. So, we will respect that and not go there."

"Mitch still lazy and old."

"Okay, I'll give you that, but don't push it." Mitch said, elbowing Felipe.

Paco and Mitch laughed. The surrounding boys nodded and wondered about getting back into the water for the next set of waves.

"You and others been very good for the boys." Paco said.

"It's been very good for us, too, Paco."

"This the last trip for Mitch and others?" Paco asked.

Mitch spun seaweed between his thumb and index finger. Lifted his head towards the sea. His eyes seemed glazed. He swallowed hard. Coughed at a slight stabbing pain in his chest. "Maybe, Paco. Maybe."

Three

They missed their original departure day. Something about the best waves ever.

Missed again the next day. Some lame excuse about leftover food and something in the wind telling Mitch perfect waves were coming.

Perfect waves!

That and Raul wanted to show Mitch he was ready to try a three sixty. Which he was, so he and Raul sat on their boards out beyond the breakers.

"He's gonna stay another day, isn't he?"

"Yep." Mumbled Mondo, glaring down at the surf from where they sat in the dunes. He dropped the empty water bottle into their small garbage can. Pulled out another. The day was hot, the bottled water warm, but no one was complaining. The big man shaded his eyes from the setting sun, an hour before it would dip into the Pacific Ocean.

"That Raul he's with?"

"Yep."

Pounder dropped onto the sand. Also took a bottle of warm water. "He say how long?"

"Nope."

"Can't pull himself away."

"Nope."

"We gotta get on the road home. Two days late now."

"Yep." Dog said, not too concerned.

"We won't be leavin' tonight."

"Nope."

"Hate to drag him away. He loves those boys like his own."

"He does."

Stringer appeared over the crest of the dune. Surfboard under his skinny arm. He glanced back at the beach. At the distant point. Eyed the perfect waves coming up behind Mitch and Raul. "Mitch's still out there with Raul. Waitin' for the right wave for a three sixty. We're here another night. Right?"

"Yep."

"The other boys are on the beach waiting for him. He can't leave 'em alone."

"Nope."

"We can't either."

"Nope."

They looked at one another. Three of the men shrugged.

Stringer turned back towards the surf. "That being the case, if you'll excuse me, I'm gonna hit the surf with a few of my best Ejido Chapala friends."

The others slammed the last of their respective waters. Retrieved their boards and followed the lanky man back to the beach.

"Two boys are missing." Mondo said, counting heads as they made their way to the water's edge.

"I saw their parents take 'em home." Stringer said.

"Felipe still down there?"

"Yep. In the ankle busters waitin' for Mitch and Raul. That kid hates to get outta the water."

"He was carvin' more today than I've ever seen him."

Dog stopped at the top of the dune before the beach. "Mitch and Raul are waiting for a wave. Hope Raul learns to be patient for the right one. If he gets overconfident, careless, he'll eat it. We should help with the others before it's too dark."

"Too late for anything serious tonight. Mitch doesn't like the boys surfing after the sun goes down."

"*Hah!* But Mitch would surf in a cave after midnight."

"He would."

"That's a fact."

"You know what I mean. He doesn't *encourage* the boys to surf after the sun sets." Growled Stringer.

"What about when we're no longer down here?"

"That's why Mitch tries to make some rules." Shrugged Pounder. "Why he has Paco keep the boards locked up."

"Won't keep a *real* surfer from surfin'." Dog said.

They all shrugged agreement. Ambled to the water.

Four

Mitch and Raul sat atop their respective surf boards. Mitch once again explained the nuances of a three sixty. One modest wave after another lifted them, then rolled on towards the beach. All were perfectly good waves, but Mitch wanted Raul to pick *his* wave. Raul, now twenty, suffered from Down syndrome. His condition was mild, but he had a very short attention span. Things needed to be repeated. He was aggressive and very strong. As a result, Mitch had taught Raul to harness the mixed feelings and let it out on the waves.

"Take it slow, Raul." Mitch repeated as they sat on their boards waiting through the set of small waves.

On the next wave, Raul started as if to catch it. It was too small.

"No, Raul. Too small. Back down!" Mitch yelled.

He did.

"What do we call a small wave?" Mitch asked.

"A bummer." Raul said. His impatience was palpable.

"Yeah, that works." Mitch chuckled. *His* patience endless.

Mitch saw his buddies enter the water to join the other five boys. He waved. Knew he'd pressed his luck to stay longer and in doing so, forced his four friends to remain with him. He knew they really didn't mind, but, like himself, they all had families back in the states. It was time to go and he knew it.

"You ready?" Mitch yelled across the water to Raul.

The boy nodded.

They studied the next set. Mitch decided the third wave in the set would be perfect for Raul.

"You see one in the next set?" Mitch asked.

Raul shaded his eyes from the low sun. "Yes." He pointed at the third wave.

"*Yes!* Catch that one."

He did.

A perfect run to the beach. An explosive three sixty. Everyone cheered. Paco stood in the sand to applaud. Mitch caught the next wave. His smile said a lot about how he felt for Raul and the others.

"Sorry, guys. I . . ."

Pounder cut him off. "We know, Mitch. It's cool."

Mitch smiled, as did Felipe, now huddled up next to Mitch. "One more?" The small boy asked. His little face smaller than usual. A faint sadness glazed his dark brown eyes with the impending departure of Mitch and his surfing buddies.

Mondo motioned for Mitch to take Felipe back out. Mitch nodded with a smile. Mouthed a thank you. He and Felipe paddled off.

The sun disappeared beneath the horizon.

Now far enough out, beyond the breakers, Mitch and Felipe sat on their boards. "You did good today, Felipe."

Felipe nodded with a sliver of a grin. He was small for his age. Strong, lean. As a small child, an untreated high temperature scorched Felipe's brain. Left him as an eight year old forever. He spoke little. Loved all the men.

Mostly the gray-bearded, ever smiling Mitch.

And did he ever love surfing.

Mitch, like his other sixty-something buddies, felt the same for all of the boys he and his friends chose to spend their summer vacations with. Besides surfing lessons, Mitch and the others taught the special needs boys of Ejido Chapala the finer points of the English language, simple manners, honesty and the virtues of hard work and good moral values. And basic math. This was the fifteenth consecutive summer visit to the small Baja village. Not all the boys were from Ejido Chapala, only Felipe and Manny. It started with just two, but when word slowly spread across the parched sands about gentle Americans who surfed, the others appeared from small villages or one of the many scattered shacks in the hills between Highway 1 and the ocean. None had ever surfed until the five men from across the border stopped to try the waves and kept coming back.

By profession, Mitch was a special education teacher in San Diego. Helping and understanding the needs for these boys was second nature to him.

And extremely rewarding.

Mitch loved his wife and family more than anyone could ever describe. They supported him in all the crazy things he did. But he was a surfer. First and foremost. Salt water ran in his veins.

A special ed teacher a close second.

He loved drawing the two together.

"You're improving more each day, Felipe."

Felipe nodded. His gaze fixed on his friend.

"We have to leave tomorrow."

Tears immediately welled up. Felipe's head dropped to his chest.

"I will miss you as always." Mitch said.

All of you. Mitch thought.

"Miss you." Felipe said, looking up to meet Mitch's warm eyes.

"Will you surf alone, Felipe?"

"No."

Sure you will.

"Why not surf alone?"

"Danger." Felipe frowned.

"Yes. We never surf alone."

Felipe shook his head.

I know you will. I *sure would.*

"Surfing alone scares your mother. Yes?"

"Yes. Danger."

Scares me, too.

Mitch knew when to stop. He also knew Felipe would surf alone. His mother told Mitch the boy body surfed at dawn. Surfed with a board in the afternoon. Where he got the board, she did not know, but when the sun was high, he was out beyond the breakers. It worried her.

"Mitch come back?" Felipe asked.

"*Dude!* Of course."

"Dude." Felipe's smile was brighter than the sun before it set.

Before tears revealed his heart.

"Watch the sets, Felipe. You tell me which wave." Mitch said.

Felipe nodded, turned to the waves approaching. Squinted to study them.

Mitch admired Felipe. He knew this quiet little beach, the surrounding dunes, might be all the boy ever knows. Felipe's muscles tensed. A small nod or shake of his head as he determined for himself whether a wave was suitable. Mitch would glance at the waves from time to time. As he did, he couldn't help but notice a good sized wave approaching. Would Felipe see it?

"*Honker!*" Howled Felipe.

He saw it.

He was flat on his board. Swung towards the beach and began his paddle. Caught the crest and was gone.

"*Yahoo!*" Shouted Mitch. He caught the next one.

Standing in the shallows with the others, Mitch shouted to Felipe. "How was that one?"

"*Kowabunga!*" Screeched the small boy.

They all laughed until it became clear this was the end of the day's surfing. And the last day the Americans would be there to teach them. After the brief celebration, sadness struck them all.

"Boys, listen up." Mitch said. "We have to be on our way home tomorrow."

"We'll be back." Dog said.

"Yep. All of us." Stringer added.

They weren't convincing.

Felipe and Raul clung to Mitch. The others gathered around one or more of the American surfers.

Five

As was their routine, the evening before their departure back up the coast to the California border, the five die-hard surfers put on a fun party for the boys and their families. Usually soda pop, beer and lots of Mexican food.

Mitch sat under a palapa back from the big fire in the sand. Felipe's mother, Marlena, and Paco sat with him. She was an older woman, a widow. Felipe her only child.

Felipe, Raul and Jose danced and chanted around the fire. It was a rare day they had a soda pop. A true luxury for them. Mitch couldn't help but notice the thin smile on Marlena's face as she examined her son laugh and play. His uncontrolled joy.

She turned to Mitch. "Felipe happy."

"Yes, he is." Mitch said.

"A *good* boy." She said, her English much improved over the years.

"A good boy. But no surf when no Mitch."

She saddened.

"He surfs, doesn't he?"

"Yes."

"Alone."

She nodded.

"Very dangerous." Mitch insisted.

They don't get it. He thought. *How insignificant they were in the ocean's grand scheme of things.*

She cringed at the thought of Felipe not returning from the sea some morning after surfing alone. Mitch could see she was scared and struggling. Knew down deep she understood the risk, but only wanted her son to be happy. He turned to face her more.

"Do the best you can to make sure he's not alone. Even someone watching from the beach is better than him out there in the surf by himself."

She nodded. Mitch not sure she fully understood.

Mondo handed Mitch a platter of warm tortillas, chile rellenos, enchiladas and something brown and soupy in a bowl.

"What's in the bowl?" Mitch asked, swirling the oily mix.

"You worried?"

Mitch held the bowl close, eying the contents.

"Anything looking back?" Stringer asked.

"*Duh!*" Mitch said. "C'mon. What is this?"

"Not completely sure, Mitch." Mondo said. "Stir it and there's hunks of something floating around. 'Member, Big Guy, these folks don't eat Americanized Mexican food. That bowl is the kinda stuff they eat every day."

Mitch tipped the bowl up and slurped a mouth full.

Grimaced.

Smiled at Marlena. She may have made it.

"Soup." She said.

Mitch smiled, struggled to swallow, then shoved a tortilla into his mouth.

"You come back?" She asked Mitch.

"Yes. Next year if all goes well." He said. He paused, felt like the tortilla was hung up midway down his throat. He choked, swallowed and it cleared.

"What couldn't go well?" Asked Pounder, settling in with an enormous platter of food.

Abruptly, Mitch turned and threw up. Choked. Clutched his neck.

The soup?

"Sheesh, Mitch. You okay?" Asked Pounder. Mondo set his food down and crawled over.

"Y-yeah. I think so. Helluva time swallowing. Hurts a little."

"Indigestion?" Mondo said.

"Probably." Mitch said.

He didn't eat any more of his dinner. Just drank water. That, too, was hard to swallow.

The festivities lasted well into the night. The boys reluctant to leave the men. Finally, the fire out, everyone disappeared into the dark for their homes or VW campers or a mat in the sand. Mitch grabbed his sleeping bag, shoved the palapa deeper into the sand and curled up to sleep.

Seemed only minutes later he awoke to someone screaming his name.

"*Mitch! Mitch!*"

It was Marlena, Dog and Stringer. Then Mondo and Pounder joined them.

"What is it?" Mitch asked.

"Felipe." Stringer said. His Spanish was quite good. He understood Marlena's rantings. "She says he's gone. So's his board."

"Crap."

Mitch jumped to his feet, crunching his head into the low palapa. "*Damn!*"

He grabbed at his chest. Still hurt some.

To the east, the earliest, faint hint of the sun. A drab gray on the distant horizon. Mitch ran from the palapa, grabbed his board and stumbled through the dunes for the surf, scanning the breakers all the time. Too dark to see anything.

Too dark to be surfing alone.

"What else did she say, Stringer?"

"Something about the island."

"Crap!"

"Dude. You think Felipe's paddling for No-Name Island?"

"Yep."

"Why now? Why not with one of us anytime the last three weeks?"

Mitch looked at Stringer in the gloom. Behind them, all the others joined the run to the water. A couple more of the boys raced far behind." 'Cause I *wouldn't* take him out there. Told him it was too far and dangerous. I wanted him to think it couldn't be done so he wouldn't try it alone."

"Bummer." Hushed Dog from behind.

"Yeah. Major bummer." Mitch said. "I have to go find him."

"What if he's not out there?"

"Not thinking about that."

"You want us to go with you?"

"I'm good." Mitch said, starting for the surf.

"Could mean we'll be here another day." Shouted Mondo.

"Could." Mitch yelled.

"Bummer." Dog said, a grin flashed across his face.

Six

Mitch knew the water. Knew the tides, currents and swells. Knew some of the fish by name. Knew No-Name Island was a little over a miles out from the beach. Small cove and beach on the side facing the Baja shore. The rest of the island was barnacle crags, rocks and steep cliffs. If Felipe was there, he'd most likely be on or near the beach.

Mitch was hoping Felipe would see him and paddle out to join him.

No such luck.

Mitch sat up on his board halfway there. Turned to watch the sun sneak through a distant valley before completely revealing itself. He never tired of it.

Taking his time, now not far from the small island, he sat again on his board in the tiny, overlapping waves entering the small cove.

"*Felipe!*"

The water lapped. A group of gulls scolded him.

"Felipe. Where are you?"

A small, black mop of hair crept up from behind a gnarly boulder.

Felipe waved. No smile.

Mitch paddled in a little further, then slid off his board.

Felipe had sunk back behind his rock.

Mitch felt a little red in the face. Anger. He had to stow that. Set it aside. He wasn't mad at Felipe. Worried and scared was more like it. Felipe was a good boy. Knew right from wrong most of the time. Felipe loved Mitch like he would his own father. He hated to see Mitch go and did something like this every year to delay the inevitable.

The anger gone from his neck and shoulders, Mitch stowed his board and walked up the sand to the boulder. Steam no longer emanated from his ears and nostrils. Mitch slunk down to the sand on the opposite side of Felipe's boulder.

"What did we say?"

No reply.

"About surfing alone."

"Mitch not mad?"

Mitch struggled to contain a burst of laughter. *Hell, yes I'm mad.*

The kid was clever. Played every card with the careful strategy of a shark in Vegas. "No. Not mad. Disappointed."

"Disapp . . .?"

"Means, um, means you didn't do what you and I agreed."

"Felipe miss Mitch."

Played a card from up his sleeve.

"But you left your mother and went out alone. We agreed *no surfing alone.*"

"No surf."

Of course you didn't. Trump card!

"Okay. You *paddled* alone."

"Yes."

"Ya got me there, Little Buddy. C'mon around here."

"Little Buddy" Felipe repeated. "Mitch mad?"

"No way. Mad at my surfing buddy?"

"No way?"

"No way."

Without another word, Felipe appeared from behind the boulder and slouched down next to Mitch. Close enough so they touched. Mitch swung an arm around the boy's shoulders. Though he was twenty-three years old, he was small. His shoulders were small. Shuddered some.

"How was it?" Mitch asked.

"Fun."

"Dark, huh?"

"Yes. Scary."

"Told you. Would you do it again."

"Yes."

"*No!*" Mitch barked. "You said it was scary. How do you think it was for your mother? She was worried. Very scared for you."

"Felipe sorry."

"I know you are. But be sure to hug your mother and tell *her* you are sorry."

"Mitch no leave."

"Mitch has to leave, Felipe. I have a beautiful wife at home waiting for me. She's a little worried and scared, too."

Felipe turned to Mitch. "Why her scared?"

"Like your mother, she's worried every day I'm down here. She misses me."

"So, you leave today?"

"Soon 's you and me finish surfin' our way back to shore."

"Mitch no mad?"

"No. Mitch understands."

Your mother? That's another story.

"Race?"

"Sure."

Felipe was in the water before Mitch could stand up. It took a while. They paddled back towards shore and then waited for a good wave to surf to the beach. Marlena was frantic. She yelled, scolded and took a swipe at Felipe. All the while the small boy glowed his appreciation to Mitch.

Mitch winked at him and slid into the side door of the waiting bus. Dog was driving. Stringer had driven off only minutes before.

Felipe and the other boys chased behind for a while, then tired and stopped to watch the dust trail towards Highway 1.

An hour later, only Felipe remained in the middle of the road. Standing. Crying.

Seven

As always, the drive north on Highway 1 was an adventure. Especially in two, 60's VW buses as restored as budgets would allow. It wasn't that the five men couldn't afford a new, monster SUV to haul them and their boards and gear – it was just part of the surfing gig.

The years had slowed them some. Weathered their skin. Grayed their hair and beards. All had adult children. Grandchildren.

Prescriptions they thought they'd never take.

Diets to keep them regular.

And patience.

Enjoyed the little things more, like driving up old Highway 1 at thirty-five miles an hour.

Even warm water from a bottle.

And a smooth sounding VW bus.

It was all part of the gig.

His eyes watery as he contemplated leaving Felipe and the others for another year, Mitch hushed to Dog. "We should stay a night on the beach south of town?"

"Yeah." Said Dog.

The beach outside and south of Ensenada proper.

All those surfer dudes and dudettes.

Sit in the sand and reminisce when Ensenada was a much smaller town. When beer was suspicious, tequila had worms and the street vendors carried guns. When parties and drinks at the Bajia Hotel were a standard routine every day. The Bahia. Such a dump. Hulking two-story, crumbling cement structure on the beach. A pool sat outside at the center of the hotel. Always things floating in it. Stuff you wouldn't dare join.

Building opened to the beach where a gaggle of VW buses, vans and cars crushed together on the high dunes between the hotel and the water. Surfers and surfer wanna-be's called *posers*, littered in, on and under the vehicles. Sex, pot and booze the order of the day.

The crowd back then was very young. Forty years ago. Much younger than the weary five gray-beards traveling back to San Diego. A hopeful party that consisted of five old guys, warm beer and early to bed.

"We need to eat." Mondo growled.

Because of an appetite only a humpback whale could understand, the buses stopped at a small restaurant in San Vicente to feed Mondo. Las Coronas catered to the American appetite, but lingering beneath the homemade chips and spicy jalapeño salsa, an authentic taste could be found nowhere else. Mondo purred like a cat.

Albeit, a famished mountain lion.

"Feel better?" Pounder asked the big man after he'd consumed two combo plates of food.

He nodded. "Beached."

"Mitch. Not hungry?"

"Throat's sore. Little heartburn. Cold water's fine for now."

"That soup?"

Mitch nodded. "Maybe." Sipped his ice water.

"Slow road ahead for Ensenada. You want anything to go?" Dog asked Mitch.

Mitch declined. Mondo ordered a burrito-to-go in a plastic container.

They gassed the buses and headed north.

Though not far in miles, Highway 1 was slow going and the VW's were hardly race cars.

But they *were* part of the gig.

In the 60's and 70's, Ensenada was a quiet little town for American tourists who didn't want to travel too far into Baja, but still wanted to enjoy the Mexican culture and food.

Not so much anymore.

Now the third largest town in Baja, California, Ensenada boasted nearly three hundred thousand people. It was a cruise ship destination, produced wines to challenge the Napa Valley vineyards and best of all, it was warm year-round. Still, the odd vehicles with boards and wide-eyed surfers crowded the beaches, just no longer where the hotels were.

The crumbling Bahia was long since a pile of dust.

Dog pulled off Highway 1 south of the downtown. A dusty, dirt road south of the airport that led to the beach.

Almost to the beach.

They were promptly greeted by the multitude of surfers and beach bunnies who maintained the surfing culture, albeit, far from where it all began so long ago.

Mitch slid from the passenger door to cheers and hellos from so many tan bodies. Some his age, most much younger.

Now's when I wish Sandy was here. He thought.

A well-built young man approached. His smile white as bleached ivory. "Another summer with the boys?"

"Yep."

"How'd it go?"

"It went."

"Cool."

"How's the surf here?"

"Bitchin'."

"Cool. We'll join you."

"Not today, Mitch." Said a voice from behind him. Mitch turned.

"*Jetty!*"

"Hi, Mitch."

"Not today? What's up?" Mitch asked.

"Shore breaks." Jetty laughed.

"Well, at least the ocean's still there to gawk at."

"Yeah, we'll always have that. You wanna warm beer?"

"No. I'll pass." Mitch said.

They pulled the buses closer to the surf amongst the other buses and vans. Some VW's had more rust than metal, but no one minded. The line of old buses was something to see. Here and there, a VW bug, rigged to hold surf boards, one with an attached lean-to to sleep under.

All part of the gig.

Settled, Mitch kicked sand as he walked down to the water. Breakers were small. Water like glass. No wind. Gulls, the salt smell, music he hated in the background. *Rap has no place at the beach.* And a bottle of warm water.

He sat. He had the ocean. It was all he ever needed, really. Who could ask for more? He sat alone taking it all in. Felt a wave of melancholy break over him.

Where'd that come from?

Yes, as always at this time, he was missing Sandy. Looked forward to getting home. Seeing her smile. Her genuine interest in his trip and surfing with the young boys. He knew she understood. Loved that about her. He worried some about his gurgling stomach. The steady chest pain. Had never felt anything like it before.

"You want company?" Jetty asked.

"Sure."

They sat. Mostly quiet. Reflecting on the moment. Probably flashing back at brief times they'd shared. Jetty and Mitch had met in Ensenada many times over the years. Surfed together at this very beach. Only time they ever saw one another. Jetty was a hammer and nail guy from El Centro. Came to Ensenada twice a year to surf. Was damn good, too. He and Mitch often sat alone, talking. Family. Jobs. Retirement. Aches and pains.

Mostly the ocean and surfing.

"You look tired, Mitch."

"Getting old."

"Nah. I mean, pale-like tired."

"Sore throat. May have had some bad soup."

"Was it looking back at you?"

They laughed. "Surf smells good today." Mitch said.

"Does. How long you guys here?"

"Just the night. You wanna join us for dinner?"

"Gringo's?" Jetty asked.

"Sure."

"We'll walk up the beach."

"Bitchin'."

"Do you guys really still talk like that?" Mitch asked.

"Sure."

"Right on."

"Far out."

At sunset, Mitch was still chatting with Jetty. Pounder and the others, along with three other gray beards, joined them for the walk to Gringo's. A Mexican restaurant on the water that catered to the American palate. Meaning steaks, BBQ chicken, ribs and Bud Lite.

They sat together at a low table under canvas palapas in the sand. Mitch's throat was feeling a little better. Ordered chicken. Nibbled at it cautiously. A few ordered Mexican.

Mondo ordered one of everything.

His buddies were all glad to see Mitch eating again. Must have been just a bug of some sort.

Or soup with eyes.

After three hours of crack-of-dawn surfing, the men packed it up and started the trip for the border. It was only ninety miles back to San Diego, but took well over two hours. And the stop at the border was unpredictable.

Mitch would be in Sandy's arms by seven that evening.

He loved Sandy.

Her smile. Twinkly eyes. Soft neck.

All those little intangibles.
She was his BeeBee.
His BeeBee would think her Mitch looked pale.

Eight

From the curb in front, Mitch and Sandy's stucco home appeared small. The lot was narrow. Concrete steps and porch. Long vertical windows either side of the front door. Comfy, tidy, but small. Very long driveway. Led to more than just the garage way in back.

Sandy heard the unmistakable sound of a VW bus at the curb. She raced from the front door. Hugged Mitch with a short kiss, then hugged Dog for getting Mitch home safely. Then hugged her husband all the way into the house. A moment later, his small bag and surfboard safely inside, Mitch slumped onto the living room couch. Sandy brought in the tall glass of ice water he'd requested.

She was bubbly as a just opened bottle of champagne.

They sat.

She was eager for details of every day since he'd left just over three weeks earlier.

Mitch was not so eager. With his eyes closed, head resting on the back of the couch, Sandy on the edge of the coffee table in front of him, they waited for the other to start. With both her hands, she clutched one of his. His other hand clung to the cold water.

"Good trip?" She giggled.

"Yep."

"Just yep?"

"Yep."

"You okay?"

"Tired. Long drive. Too long at the border. Feel like shit."

Sandy released his hand and like any mother would with a sick child, she held the back of her hand to Mitch's forehead.

"Little warm." She said.

"It's eighty five out." His words were soft, muffled.

"You're a little red, too."

"Sore throat for a day or two. Seems to be gone now."

Liar. She thought. Now concerned.

"You look pale, Mitch."

He said nothing.

"And it looks like you lost weight."

"We surfed a ton."

"You always come back ten pounds heavier." She insisted, now getting a little worried. Mitch didn't look good.

"I'm older."

How does that matter?

"Tell me about this sore throat. I mean, you were in the sand in Mexico for weeks. Lord only knows what you could catch in those dunes."

"Not so much a sore throat as it hurts to swallow."

Crap!

"Hurt bad?"

"Didn't at first. Does now."

She knew it, he was denying. Wouldn't admit a tough surfer dude could get sick.

"We should go see the doctor."

Mitch turned to the love of his life. "Okay. You're the mom here. 'Sides, it's been getting worse each day. First it seemed like a sore throat. You know, hard to swallow. Now it *hurts* to swallow."

"A lot?"

"Yes."

"*Sheesh, Mitch!* Should have come home sooner."

"Only been a couple days since it began. Couldn't have been home much sooner."

"I'll call Scanlon's office." Sandy said.

Reluctantly, Mitch nodded.

She was back in minutes. "Tomorrow at ten unless you feel it's urgent enough to go to the E.R."

"No. I'm good until morning." He said, his head back, eyes closed again.

He drifted off.

Sandy stood, hands on hips studying her Mitchell. He was tan as usual, in a pale way. Scruffy, three-day growth where he normally shaved to keep his thick, nearly white beard, tidy. He was only sixty-four. Handsome in an incredibly cute way. A smile that charmed. Eyes that slivered when he smiled. She worried about him.

She covered him with a light sheet. Drew the front window shades. Planned no dinner.

Sandy kissed Mitch's forehead, pressed the back of her hand on it again. Shook her head. Slipped to the back of the house where she began phoning their three adult children. They always wanted to know about their dad's surfing trip and know he'd gotten home safe.

But with each call and each carefully worded explanation of Mitch's sore throat, Sandy's anxiety grew. After the last call to their son, Mitchell, but not Mitchell Jr., Sandy decided ten in the morning was to long to wait.

Am I being crazy here? She wondered.

She tiptoed back to the living room. Mitch had thrown up.

Looked up at Sandy. He was rubbing his chest. "Feels like Satan himself has lit a fire behind my sternum."

"I'll get my keys." Sandy said.

"Okay."

Nine

The E.R. was crazy busy when they arrived. A kid and his girlfriend lost control of his motorcycle. They collided head-on with a family visiting San Diego on vacation. Going to Sea World.

The kid driving the bike died instantly. His fifteen-year old girlfriend died shortly after in the Emergency Room.

Mid August in San Diego, those hell-bent last days before school started, were crazy like summer break in Fort Lauderdale.

Sandy helped Mitch sit down in the waiting room.

The visiting family of five heading for Sea World each sustained minor scrapes and bruised. Might not make it to Sea World, but would be released as soon as the E.R. doctors agreed to let them go.

Lots of crying and screaming and scared people.

"Makes my swallow problem not so important." Mitch said.

"Don't kid yourself, Surf Bum." She said. "You have something that's not right."

"Surf Bum?"

"*Mondo* Surf Bum."

"Not sure Mondo would appreciate that." Mitch said, mustering a weak smile.

Sandy abruptly stood. Marched around the waiting room like a drill sergeant. Came to a halt in front of the slouching Mitch. "You're not taking this serious, Mitchell."

He knew he wasn't. "No, I'm not." He said, not making eye contact. "I've been sick before. Probably be all well tomorrow."

"Can you take it serious until then?"

"Sure."

"For me."

He looked up, "Of course."

"Mitchell, I mean it!"

"I can tell. You never call me Mitchell."

"Damn it, Mitchell!"

Took another hour plus before a nurse approached with a clipboard and a pile of forms. Sat next to Mitch. He looked awful.

"So," The nurse started.

Mitch puked all over her clipboard.

"So," She continued, hardly losing a beat. "Something upsetting your stomach."

She was very cool Mitch thought. He knew Dog would have said she was *bitchin'*.

"Not so much the stomach. More the throat. Can't swallow very well. Hurts like hell." Mitch said.

"He says he has heartburn in his chest." Sandy added.

"All this going on in your esophagus?"

He looked at the nurse for clarity.

"Is the discomfort up and down your esophagus versus in your stomach?"

Mitch thought. "Sure."

The nurse made notes.

"No blood in that vomit. Has there ever been any?"

"No." Mitch looked at Sandy.

Blood?

"That's good." The nurse said. "I'll confer with the doctor. Be right back." She left them to ponder blood in Mitch's vomit.

Sandy took Mitch's face between her palms and moved up close. Nose to nose. "Any blood? Ever?"

He shook his head.

"Good."

Apparently *be right back* meant later that night. But when she finally did return, the nurse didn't come alone. A very big, tan man followed her. "I'm Doctor Rodin." He extended his hand. Like the rest of him, it, too, was large. "I've called doctor Scanlon and he'll be here shortly. I'd like to do an EGD."

"Huh?"

"Endoscopy."

"For my throat you're going up my ass?" Mitch asked, alarmed.

Doctor Rodin shook his head, not amused. "No. A flexible tube down your throat. Like to examine the wall of your esophagus."

Doctor Scanlon arrived. Nodded at Rodin and squeezed in to sit between Mitch and Sandy. "So, word has it we're heading for an EDG." He was smiling. Knew Mitch well. Put a hand on Mitch's leg. Turned to him.

Mitch heaved a bubbly substance across Scanlon's starched, white lab coat. Scanlon stopped speaking, looked down at the red and green stripe splashed across his mid section. Looked up at Rodin.

"Let's get this done, pronto."

Sandy was already fighting back the tears.

Blood! We didn't need blood.

Mitch turned a brighter shade of pale. The nurse and Doctor Rodin helped him into a wheelchair. Sandy kissed Mitch on the cheek. Whispered into his ear she loved him.

"I'm taking it serious now, BeeBee." Mitch said, trying to be glib. "I love you too much."

And he was gone down the hall. Sandy watched them disappear through double doors. She thought there appeared to be a sense of urgency in how fast they wheeled him.

Damn! She started punching speed dial numbers into her cell phone.

The EDG gave the docs two things. An ugly view of Mitch's esophagus and a biopsy. The biopsy would take time to evaluate, but Rodin's response to the ugly view wasn't encouraging.

He'd seen enough cancer to know the biopsy was probably not necessary.

Sandy stood behind Mitch in his wheelchair.

"Won't mince words." Rodin said. Scanlon stood back listening. "It's cancer and it's advanced."

Sandy gasped. Mitch hung his head. A cold sweat burst from every pore.

"We'll need to move quickly, Mitch. Sandy." Scanlon added, looking from one to the other and back at Mitch.

"I'm scheduling a CT scan *immediately*." Rodin said. He nodded at the nurse who promptly pushed Mitch down the hall to another imaging room.

Immediately meant a two hour wait on a gurney in the hall outside the imaging room. Sandy dragged a chair to the head of the gurney where Mitch and she could talk. Outside, the August day turned to August night.

Hot August Night. Thought Sandy. *Neil Diamond.* Her mind raced over the years she and Mitch had shared. The surfing. The kidding. The laughs. *The Beach Boys.* Their tiny wedding on surfboards in the water off Mission Bay Park. They were so young. *Dick Dale.* Mitch, a mop-haired surfer, callouses and knots up and down his legs and feet. She more into Mitch than the surfing. *The Rendezvous Ballroom in Balboa.* Trips to Mexico for the *best waves ever.* The birth of their children. *The Ventures.* Mitch's work with Special Olympics. He always thought they needed a surfing competition. *Eddie & the Showmen.*

Now here they were, in a dim hall waiting for bad news. Sandy sobbed. Held Mitch's hand. He squeezed hers. Knew what she was thinking. All those good times.

A young man, more of a kid, opened the CT scan room door. A lady, crying, clung to her husband as they exited the room.

"Are you Mitch?" He asked.

"Yep."

"I'll be ready for you in a minute."

Mitch and Sandy nodded at the same time.

Few minutes later the young man returned, and they all went inside. The kid turned to them, "Because the CT scan cannot tell us how big a mass is over one centimeter, we need to determine the extent of your cancer. Positron emission tomography, or PET, will help us know more. If necessary, we'll follow up with an ultrasound."

Sandy shook her head. "So much. Isn't there just one test or scan or something, that can tell you what you need to know?"

"No, Ma'am. Each leads to the next. If the first told us everything, you wouldn't be here now."

"It's okay, Sandy." Mitch said.

She nodded.

Two hours later Mitch and Sandy were waiting for an ultrasound.

Mitch slept on the gurney. Sandy was asleep on a couch across the from him. It had been a long day for them both. Shortly after midnight, both Rodin and Scanlon entered the small waiting room. Sandy woke immediately. "What?" She yelped, jumped to her feet to join them.

Mitch woke. Turned his head to the threesome standing in the middle of the room.

"And don't mince." Mitch said.

"Won't." Rodin said. He looked less than optimistic.

"Serious?" Mitch asked.

"Yes."

The doctors sat. Shared all they'd learned the last twelve hours.

"Tumor's big. By this time tomorrow you may not be able to swallow at all." Rodin said.

"So," Mitch struggled to swallow his own saliva, "The stent will allow some swallowing, but this esopha . . . esophag . . ."

"Esophagectomy." Scanlon said.

"Yeah, that, will take out the tumor and get me back on a surfboard, when?"

Scanlon dropped his head.

"Oh, Mitch." Sandy cried.

"An esophagectomy will remove the tumor and part of your esophagus. Move your stomach up more into your chest cavity. Recovery won't allow surfing."

"Ever?" Mitch stiffened.

"Possibly."

Scanlon stepped closer. "Mitch, you have what we call stage four-B esophageal cancer. Means it's moved rapidly from your esophagus to surrounding lymph nodes and other organs."

"What about the stent thing you were discussing?" Sandy blurted out.

"Mitch is too far along for a stent to be the answer all by itself. We can do the stent, but he needs aggressive chemo and surgery and everything else we can do."

Mitch was quiet.

Sandy and the two doctors chatted as if he wasn't in the room.

His boys. Felipe. Raul. And Paco. Crap! Thought Mitch.

He listened. Sandy's voice quivered. She was scared.

"How long?" Mitch asked.

The three turned to him.

"We can start chemo immediately." Scanlon said. Rodin nodded.

"No." Mitch gagged. Sandy huddled up to him.

"Mitch, we have to start treatments."

"The stent." Mitch whispered.

"The stent will relieve your symptoms and improve your quality of life."

"I'll be able to swallow?"

"Yes."

"And if that's all we do, how long would I have?"

Sandy screamed in anguish. *"No, Mitch!* We need to throw everything we can at this."

"Okay." Mitch said. He looked at the two doctors. "And if we toss everything at it?"

"It's stage four, Mitch. Few survive. Absolutely no guarantees. We could get it all, and it will most certainly return."

"A life of chemo, blood tests, scans and needles."

"Yes."

"But you'd be alive, Mitch." Sandy said through tears.

"That ain't livin'." Mitch said. "Back to my original question, how *long* with just the stent?"

"If we inserted a stent along with some aggressive chemo and internal radiation therapy, maybe three months. Longer if we did more."

"But it's gonna get me one way or another." Mitch said.

Rodin nodded. Scanlon turned away.

"Mitch." Sandy said.

He held up a hand. "Can you two leave me and BeeBee alone for a little while."

Scanlon nodded. Left the room.

Rodin lingered. "If you pray, this would be a good time."

He left.

Ten

"Pray?" Mitch said.

Sandy nodded. "Don't worry about prayer, Mitch. I'll do that for the both of us."

He dropped his head. He never could get his long, tan arms around Christianity. Always mumbled something about it all being so hard to believe. "Sorry. Jury's still out on your friend in the sky."

"I know."

"If He was all you say He is, why is this happening to me?" Mitch whined.

"You really want to go there?" Sandy asked.

"No."

"Good, 'cause I'm *always* ready."

Mitch thought a moment. Recognized the soft stuff he was stepping into and hastily changed the subject.

"So, what do you think about treatment?" Mitch asked.

"I think you should go for it all and see if it buys you more time."

"I'm not so sure."

"Mitch, we need to fight this with all we have."

"Why?"

She fell apart. Hugged him. "I don't want you to leave me."

"Sandy." He gurgled. Fought to swallow. "The stent, and sure, a little chemo and other crap, then you, me, maybe the guys, we head for Ejido Chapala. We take our families, too. All of us. One last trip."

"*Before you die!*" She howled in tears.

Mitch hadn't thought that far ahead. Easy for him to up and die. Leave everyone behind. Sad for them. Nothing for him.

"Y-yeah, I guess so."

He's in denial.

"Mitchell, you're giving up too quickly."

"Am I?" He said. "There have been only three things in this life I've ever truly loved. Surfing, you, the kids and . . ."

"And more surfing." She finished for him. "That's four things."

"So, who's counting?"

"You are."

"I suppose. But I sure don't want you remembering me with needles poking from my arm, bald as a cue ball and gargling my food six times a day. *No!* Not gonna *wipe out* that way."

Sandy sighed. Wiped her tears. She heard him.

Heard the cry of passion in his voice. How many people ever felt so strong about something like Mitch felt about surfing? Oh, she knew it wasn't *just* the surfing. It was all of it. The *gig*, as he called it. The sea. The friends. The boards and lingo. The whole running the tube and sand thing. And the Ejido Chapala boys. He loved those kids. He'd brought so much to them and enriched their lives far beyond imagination. Yes, Mitch's passion overshadowed three months of misery and horrid goodbyes to friends and neighbors.

That wasn't Mitch.

Was she jealous?

Never! She loved the ride. Being a part of Mitch's *green room.* His sand. His wind. Catching a big one and running the barrel. His boys and endless Mexican food. *A road trip with her and his family?* Sure. And those great surfing buddies and their VW buses.

He was right.

"So you want to drop dead on your beat up long board in the barrel of a mondo wave. Yes?"

"Bitchin'." A little color had returned to his face.

"Okay. So we do the stent and some minimal other stuff and head for Baja."

For the first time in half a day, Mitch smiled. She kissed him.

"Yeah. Call the kids."

"Already did. All are on their way."

"And the guys? Mondo, Stringer?"

"I'll call them after we talk to Rodin and Scanlon." She said, looking down on Mitch with sad, but hopeful eyes.

"It's best, BeeBee." He smiled. "It's not too late for one last set of waves."

"Oh, Mitch, stop it!" She said, but knew he was serious. Kissed him and opened the door for the doctors.

They shared their decision. Their *comfort* in the decision.

Rodin, a surfer at times, completely understood. "We'll schedule the stent this afternoon. Radiation in a couple of days. But Mitch, you'll have to go slow. You won't be the hot dog you once were."

Mitch smiled at the thought.

Sandy nodded. A single tear dribbled down her soft cheek.

"Where did you say you might go?" Rodin asked.

Mitch coughed up some blood. "Tell ya, haveta kill ya."

"Waves that good?"

"Yep."

Sandy smiled at Rodin as she slipped her arm into Mitch's. "You're welcome to join us, Doc."

"No thanks. They'd have to kill me."

Eleven

The hospital put Mitch and Sandy in an inpatient room with two beds. One for each of them. Sandy was exhausted. Mitch worried he'd never surf again. Rodin scheduled the stent procedure for six hours later to allow them both time to rest. It had been a long two days.

Rest was elusive.

Mitch was flat on his back. He was not a back-sleeper, but it was the best position that allowed for any swallowing.

Sandy sat propped up as if she was reading, but only stared straight ahead in the dimly lit room. They had tried for over two hours to sleep. Sandy had mulled over in her mind all they'd heard and learned about stents, cancer, PET's and how to get hot coffee from the cafeteria. Sandy cried from time to time when her mind collated the seriousness of the situation. She muffled it from Mitch. The love of her life, her Mitch, was dying and there was nothing she or anyone else could do about it.

I'm having some doubts, Father.

She knew He was there. He was always there. In the good times and the bad.

I guess it's my turn to ask, why me?

She mulled about all those who at times like this questioned His motives. His plans for us. All the *why me* and *where is He* arguments that frustrate those who simply don't understand how He works. At this moment it was difficult for even a faithful Sandy to not be frustrated or questioning.

Then she prayed. *Oh, Father, don't misunderstand my thoughts. If You were so inclined, it would be fine with me to change this course for one without the cancer. Just* swish *it away and all will be fine by me. But if this is Your way, I ask You to make it the best You can for Mitchell.*

Mitch rustled in his bed next to her.

"You say something, BeeBee?"

She feigned being asleep.

Mitch closed his eyes picturing the next set of waves collating around No-Name Island.

Eventually, they both slept, but for only a few hours. Neither slept well.

At eleven the night of the second day, the door eased opened. Two nurses came in, one pushing a wheelchair. "Time to wake up, you two. We'd like to get that stent in so you can maybe drink a little water." She said.

Sandy woke. Nodded she was awake. Followed them until Mitch went into a surgical suite. They kissed. He smiled.

She knew he was worried, but not sure about what. The stent or pulling off a double spinner in the waves at Ejido Chapala.

While Mitch was fitted with the stent, Sandy woke their three children in the waiting room. She cried. They, too. Sandy led them to the cafeteria for coffee and something to eat. She explained what she and Mitch were going to do. And invited them and their families.

"Mom! You can't do that! He needs chemo."

"Needs rest and probably radiation."

"Why would you let him do that?"

"Yeah, why would you let him?"

"It's crazy."

Blah, blah, blah. Thought Sandy.

"Listen, you three." Sandy said. "This is *your* father. The big Kahuna. Mister surfboard. Would you want to be the ones to deny him the pleasure of what has defined his life?"

"No."

"Think of what surfing has meant to him. To us as a family. To his special ed kids here in San Diego."

"Or to those four hippie surfer dudes he hangs ten with." Laughed the daughter.

Sandy laughed, "Yes. Or those surfing-crazed special needs kids in Baja. Their little lives revolve around Mitch and the summer visits." She said. "And then there's the parade, the breakfast club and so much more."

"Mom, don't forget his infamous surfing chess tournament."

"Oh, my. What a disaster. How could I or anyone forget that!" Sandy howled.

"Hah! I know lots of people who would like to forget." They each flashed on one or more memories of the crazy antics of Mitch and his well-honed team of chess-playing surf boarders.

As if she read their collective minds, Sandy said, "You see the memories? The fun and games surfing has brought us. All because your father had a need for workin' the board."

"He sure can work a board."

"With the best of 'em."

"Bitchin'." Came a voice from the other end of the cafeteria.

They turned as one to a voice they knew all too well.

"Dad!"

Mitch sat up a little straighter in his wheelchair. His speech was clearer and he held a small glass of ice water.

"They say I need another night in this place, but if I'm really good and promise to give him surfing lessons, doc says I can go home now." Mitch said. His smile said even more.

"Then let's go."

They did.

Trip included a long, slow drive down Garnet Street to the dead end before the Crystal Pier. Sandy parked. Mitch just stared at the pier. The waves broke in, under and around the old wooden structure. Men, young and old, leaned on their forearms on the rail. A fishing pole in one hand. Beer in the other. Young surfers paddled out, caught a wave and rode in. Sandy pulled out, drove north on Bayard to Diamond then towards the water to Mission. Then back again.

"Could you just park again near the pier?" Mitch asked.

"Sure."

The kids followed in their car behind. When Sandy parked, their three adult children jumped into the back seat.

"Just like old times." Mitch said, noting the three of them behind him as if going off to school.

"Mostly." Said the son.

"What, mostly?" Sandy asked.

"Dad drooled at the sight of the ocean back then. Now he purrs."

Mitch laughed. Coughed, then choked.

"Sorry, Dad."

"You guys gonna go with us?"

Behind Mitch, the three looked at each other in a consulting manner. Daughter took the lead.. "We talked about it. Sounds like it might be better if we didn't."

Sandy turned around to face them. "Why's that? We'd all be together. Surfing together."

Their daughter, an accountant in Pacific Beach, shrugged. "We kinda think you two should spend time alone. Together."

"We'll have Mondo, Dog, Stringer and Pounder with us. Maybe their families, and then there's all Mitch's surf boys and their moms and dads. Maybe even one of Mitch's doctors. We won't be alone."

"Mom, we just think, well . . ." The daughter started to cry. Then both sons.

Emotions had been beaten. Flogged and chained. Run raw.

And no one wanted to be there when Mitch slipped off on his last wave.

"Okay." Mitch said. "You're right. This won't be a fun-packed family outing. Better you stay behind. 'Sides, we'll be back."

They sat in the car pondering that comment for a long time. Everyone thinking about what Mitch had said. He didn't sound angry. Or happy. Just . . . resigned.

The *coming back* part. Nobody touched that. No one wanted to start a conversation for fear of crying again.

"Let's go home, BeeBee." Mitch said. "Kinda tired."

Twelve

Mitch had a restless night. Sandy, too. No surprise.

The surprise came when Sandy woke around six-thirty. Surf Bum was gone. His side of the bed cold. Without shouting, she didn't want to wake their three children scattered around the house on couches and guest beds, she scuttled about the house whispering his name.

"Mitch?"

Office was empty. Bathrooms vacant. Kitchen same as it was the night before.

On a wild hunch, Sandy left out the back door, scooted along the wall to the garage and small storage building at the back of the property.

"Oh, Mitch! No!"

His board was gone.

Both cars were in the drive. The walk, though not difficult at any other time, was a long four blocks for a man with esophageal cancer and a new stent to enable him to swallow. Sally raced inside, debated whether to wake the kids.

The kids! She thought. *Hardly kids anymore.*

Decided against a crowd yelling and screaming for Mitch. She slipped into their red crossover and left for the pier. She knew his route. Drove slow enough to look for him. Fast enough to get there quickly. If he was surfing, he'd walk down Diamond, slip down to the beach and cut across to the pier to join the other surfers. If he was going to the pier, he'd cut through the parking lot along the beach, then around to the pier on Garnet.

Sandy covered it all. No Mitch. She parked in the lot and scanned the surfers. No Mitch. She looked across the beach, up to the pier.

Mitch!

Sandy chuckled to herself. Mitch, when not surfing, would go out on the pier, *precisely four hundred feet* to the first of the breakers. Where the surfers sat on their boards watching the sets come in.

She watched him from her car. His board leaning on the pier rail next to him. His animated gestures to the surfers. He knew them all. Most of them a student of his at one time or another.

A seagull shit on her windshield.

She laughed. *This* was Mitch's world. Young, tan kids eager to learn. Crashing waves and the smell of the ocean. Seagull shit. Where he was at his best. She loved that about him. So committed. So involved. So in love with it all.

Livin' the dream.

Sandy fought the urge to drive home and leave him be. The nurse in her said *no*. He needed someone nearby right now. She wanted to be with him. Enjoy his world with him. He always included her. Seemed to enjoy it all that much more when she was at his side. Sandy left the car. Strode slowly out onto the pier. About halfway to Mitch she stopped to listen to him laugh, shout and share what he knew with the youngsters below. All eager to pick Mitch's saltwater and sand brain.

Mitch suddenly laughed hard enough to cause him to buckle over. He threw up. All liquid. Kind of greenish. Sandy rushed to him. He saw her coming.

She wrapped an arm around him. Helped him straighten. Below the kids couldn't see what happened. He looked at Sandy. Smiled.

"Hi, BeeBee."

"Hi, Honey." She smiled back, doing all she could to hide her concern.

"I knew you'd know where I disappeared to."

She smiled. Nodded. "You okay?"

"Been better." He looked sad. Gray.

"What is it, Mitchell?"

"Couldn't sleep. Called each of the guys this morning."

"You woke them?"

"Yep."

"*Mitchell!*"

"Funny thing. None of them cared that I woke them."

Of course not, Beach Bum. You're dying.

"Good. I'm not surprised."

"Not a one of them wants to go with us to Ejido Chapala. *Not one!*"

"It's okay. We'll be alright." She reassured. "They're not deserting you. Must want you to . . ."

"Be alone to die by myself!"

"*Mitchell!* You know better than that."

"No one wants to watch me max out. Not the kids. Not the guys. *Shit!* Everyone's sending me off to the big bail out all by myself."

"Well, at least good old chopped liver will be along." Sandy said, glaring out over the water.

He took her shoulders. "Sorry. Guess I'm feeling sorry for myself."

She hugged him. He hugged back.

"The boys, Felipe, Renaldo, Raul, Mister Paco, all the others. They'll be crazy happy to see you."

Mitch's eyes misted up. He turned to the water. Watched a kid he didn't know catch a wave and body surf until he skidded into the sand. Then, "We don't tell anyone in Ejido Chapala."

"Okay."

"We go down, party hardy, surf until we can't walk and eat . . . *crap!*"

"What?"

"Bet I can't eat much of anything when we're there."

"Pablum."

"Soup." He said, with a smirk. He loved her wit.

"Cream of wheat."

"*Pablum?*"

"Lots of it." She laughed. Hugged him again. "We'll be fine. Easy on the enchiladas and tequila."

"Crap!"

"Eventually."

They laughed until they cried.

"How long can we keep on this mask of deception?" He asked.

"Not sure. How long you got?" She said.

"Wow! Don't know."

"Then we wear the mask as long as you want."

"Or we tell all to everyone."

"Your call, Surfer Dude."

"Everyone I know and love already knows and sworn to secrecy." He said. " 'Cept the boys."

"Then it's in your hands when to pull the trigger to tell."

"Scared."

"Why?"

"When everyone knows, it makes it more real."

"It *is* real, Mitch. Won't get any more or less real."

"I couldn't sleep thinking about you." He scowled.

"Me?"

"Alone. Without me. Never wanted that for you."

Sandy shivered. Hadn't thought of it that way. The empty bed. Single dish at dinner. The toilet seat always down. She *would* be alone.

"Never wanted to be the first to go." He added. "I know you'll be sad. Maybe even mad at me."

She wiped the tears. Struggled to lighten up. "I'll have your surfboard."

He wasn't biting.

"*No!* I mean it. It's not fair to you." He shouted.

"Or you."

"Hell, BeeBee, I'll be dead. What will I care?"

Again, Sandy veered away from the sadness. She wanted so desperately to maintain calm and acceptance. "You gonna surf this morning?"

"I could."

"No, Mitch. Rodin warned you about too much. Carrying your board down here was too much."

" 'Spose."

"Let's get home. I'm calling everyone we know to tell them we're outta town on vacation. The kids are going home, but will return when we do."

"We?"

"When *we* return." She emphasized.

"Okay." He said, suddenly looking older and very tired.

"Then I'll call Paco and let him know we're coming down. The boys will be thrilled about a second visit from Mister Mitch in one year."

"I sure hope I don't keel over and . . ."

Sandy raised a hand to interrupt, "Time to climb up onto your optimistic board, Surfer Guy. You won't. I won't let you."

God, please help me!

Their hug was long. Heartfelt. He kissed her.

One of the boys below rolling with the waves, yelled for them to get a room.

Mitch waved. Sandy smiled, shook her head, hefted his board. They walked hand in hand back to the car. Then drove home.

Thirteen

As the next two days evolved, no one accepted the invitation to go along to Ejido Chapala with Mitch and Sandy. Mostly scheduling issues and family commitments. After a long, confidential meeting with the school principal and school district superintendent, Mitch simply took a leave of absence from teaching.

Stringer loaned Mitch his VW bus.

"Hurt her and you're dead, Mitch." Stringer said, not realizing the implications of what he'd said.

"We're all gonna die some day." Mitch said, not missing a beat.

"Just be careful, Sand Bug."

"Like a kamikaze run."

"Thanks. Enjoy. See you when you get back."

"Wish you could go." Mitch said.

"Me, too. Next summer's just around the corner. Later." And Stringer drove off with his family in their Chrysler van.

Next summer? Wondered Mitch.

Sandy had been standing on the front porch during the exchange between old friends. She stepped down and hugged Mitch. "That was interesting." She said.

"Yeah." Mitch said, obviously preoccupied.

"What is it?" She asked.

"I hope we're doing the right thing keeping everyone in the dark. They could be pissed when they finally hear."

Sandy kissed his cheek. "We'll give them all the details when we return."

"What if I don't?"

"Then you won't have to worry about it. Will you?"

" 'Spose not."

"Nope."

"BeeBee, you think I'm going to Hell?"

She laughed. "Why would you ask that?"

"I'm not a believer. A Christian like you."

"You're *not* going to Hell. God loves you as He loves me. We are all His children. And other than not acknowledging Jesus as your Savior, you have lived a thoroughly righteous life, Sand Dab."

"Is it too late?"

"For Jesus?"

"Yeah."

"Never."

They packed the bus. Then drove to Doctor Rodin's office. The doctor gave Mitch a brief examination, a lecture on not over doing it and was sorry he couldn't go along. Mitch and Sandy went to the pharmacy. Picked up two prescriptions for Mitch, then drove to the end of Harrington Avenue. Parked and walked to the grass up from the sand dunes and beach. Across the open water, the pier and hundreds of surfers.

Mitch's eyes glazed over.

Lost in another world.

"I love surfing, Sandy."

"I know."

"I mean, I *really* love surfing."

"I know."

"You know, the sense of wonder as each wave rolls under you. Lifts you up. Sets you down. Was that the one? The pull of the waves. The sounds. The smells. Kelp. The incredible power the ocean exhibits in a flirtatious way. The unpredictable currents beneath. And you wait. Eying each wave as it develops towards you and the beach. Then you see it. *The* one. The adrenaline oozes from your pores. And like a well-oiled machine, you turn your board, power up your arms and begin. Then it breaks and you're off. Like a thoroughbred from the starting gates, *you're off.* Then . . ."

Sandy watched Mitch speak. His eyes reflected the ocean. At times his lips trembled with excitement. His passion consumed him.

" . . . and you finish with a flurry." Mitch concluded. He looked over at her. "Sorry."

"Oh, don't mind me, Hot Dog." She laughed. "I love how you love it."

"I love you, too."

"I know."

She stood. Helped him up. They stopped for some dinner. Mitch a milkshake. Sandy a burger and salad.

"You think I can get a milkshake in Ejido Chapala?"

"Don't know." She mulled. "Do they have milk?"

"Goats."

"A goat's milk shake?" Sandy screwed up her face.

"Maybe not." Mitch laughed.

It was good to hear Mitch laugh.

Fourteen

If Mitch and Sandy had zipped down Highway 1 in their crossover SUV, the trip to Lazaro Cardenas, just east of Ejido Chapala, would have taken six hours without stopping. But the two hundred and four miles, door to door, was no simple trip for any vehicle.

And Stringer's VW bus wasn't just any vehicle. After all, it had forty horses.

It carried a sick man aboard.

And then there was Sandy's bladder.

So, all things considered, they would spend a restful night in Ensenada, a little less than halfway.

Sandy drove the entire trip. This way she could manage her bladder stops as often as she needed. Mitch slept off and on. Moaned at bumps in the road. Only threw up once.

Next morning, they left their downtown hotel at sunrise and arrived in Lazaro Cardenas at two that afternoon. Many stops. Mitch was doing poorly. Dry heaves. Shortness of breath. The heat was intolerable.

Sandy, though nowhere near as uncomfortable as Mitch, was not doing much better. She was not a heat monger and the late summer heat was pressing up against triple digits.

"Would you like to stay in a hotel tonight in Lazaro Cardenas?" Sandy asked.

Mitch nodded he did. He was a new, grayer shade of pale. Looked pasty and unnatural like a clay sculpture of himself. He kind of looked like Mitch, but you needed a double take to be sure.

Sandy pulled into Lazaro Cardenas. Stopped in a cloud of dust outside a cantina. She went inside. Stood beneath a large ceiling fan to ask where she could find a hotel. Came out and walked across the street and into a two-story, stucco building with no obvious outside sign. As she had been told in the cantina, it was a hotel. Five rooms. She inspected the rooms first. One at a time. Took the third, the one closest to the shared bathroom.

When she returned, Mitch was white-ish green like sea foam. Sound asleep.

"*Mitch! Wake up.*" Sandy yelled as if he'd abruptly departed. "You look like shit."

"Feel more like diarrhea. You get a room?"

"Sort of. It'll do. Come on."

She helped him to the bathroom where he sat and did something he hadn't done in three days.

Flushed it down.

Some color returned to his face. He washed his hands. Slapped his cheeks to bring even more color to them. It hurt. Shuffled to their room. Sandy sat on the bed making notes about Mitch's condition. Something Doctor Scanlon requested.

"You could lie." Mitch said, collapsing on the bed.

"Could."

"Won't?"

"Nope. One look at you and a roadkill could tell I was lying. Your cancer is serious, Mitch. Assuming you *survive* this little, crazy expedition, we'll want to get into all that radiation and chemo stuff Scanlon and Rodin want for you."

"Why bother. Statistically I have less than a fifteen percent chance of living. And after this *crazy expedition,* as you call it, my chances will probably be zero."

"If you knew that, why are we here?" She glared at him.

"One last, big ass wave, BeeBee."

"All those hardened knots on your knees and feet have gone to your sand-filled head, Dune Boy." She scolded. "Me and those two doctors aren't throwing in the towel until . . ."

"I'm cold and six feet under." He said, then sat up. "Hey!"

"What?"

"What about that? My burial."

"I thought you wanted to be cremated." Sandy said.

"I do." He said. "My ashes scattered."

"I know." She said. "We've discussed this before. For both of us."

"Remind me where I wanted my ashes cast." He said.

"Where else?"

"Oh. Of course. The surf."

"*Duh!* Sand Flea."

Little did Mitch know Sandy and their three children were already pulling together information for something special for Mitch. No one had brought it up as yet. It was difficult work considering what they were planning. Often, Sandy's research ended in tears.

They slept, though the heat left them drained in the morning. The bed was wet from perspiration. For breakfast, Mitch coughed and gagged through toast soaked in goat's milk. He and Sandy kidded that maybe the goat's milk would scare the cancer away.

Swallowing was difficult. Mitch looked awful and had already lost weight. He worked a tall ice water and sips of Sandy's coffee while she was in the restroom.

He threw it all up out the VW bus window.

"We should leave that on the side of the bus for Stringer." He joked.

"We should." Sandy said. Not laughing. "It would teach him a lesson to not share with his cancer-ridden friends."

"Sandy, don't stop in town." Mitch said. "Drive through to the beach."

She did.

The road was rough from Lazaro Cardenas to Ejido Chapala. Carved out of the cliffs and rolling hills hundreds of years ago. No one was considering fancy VW buses might travel them in the future. Small lean-to huts and shacks popped up from time to time. Clothes on the line. A burro. Crude fences for critters built from whatever could be scavenged. Kids played with whatever looked like fun. Everyone looked up.

Stringer's two-tone, velvet green and white '67 bus was immediately recognized by everyone from Ejido Chapala to the Pacific Ocean, about two miles. Usually kids and some adults, ran to the road to watch it bounce along the road.

Today was no exception.

Paco couldn't resist. He rousted his son, Manny, and together they cut through the dunes and cactus for the beach. Yelling and screaming. Raul joined them.

Renaldo and Jose abandoned their makeshift soccer game to hurry cross country to the beach.

"Pull up around this grove of trees. We'll wait for the boys."

Fifteen minutes later everyone was there.

But no Felipe.

"Where's Felipe?" Mitch asked. His voice a whisper compared to what it had been.

Jose pointed to the water.

"Surfing?" Mitch scowled.

Paco stepped forward. "No. He wait for you for three days. Camp on the beach for you to arrive. No board. No surf." Paco smiled. He had kept the boards secure.

Mitch introduced Sandy to Paco and then each boy. As a tight little group, they took Mitch's surfboard and meandered through the scrub brush to the beach. Felipe sat facing the waves. His little campsite well above high tide. A pit for a fire. A lean-to. Above the whipping wind and crashing waves, he could not hear the group descend upon him.

But when he turned and saw Mitch, he exploded to his feet.

Ran like his hair was on fire until he was wrapped in Mitch's arms.

The crush of the small boy hurt enough for Mitch to stagger, clutch his stomach and chest.

The boys loved American surfer lingo. "Kowabunga, Felipe!" Mitch cried.

"Ya-hoo, Mister Mitch." Felipe howled.

"Felipe, this is my wife, Sandy."

Felipe looked her over. "This is BeeBee?"

"*Ulp!*"

"These guys know me as BeeBee?" Sandy asked with a friendly glare at Mitch.

"Yep." Mitch said. "Beach Bunny."

"I know. I know." She said. "But them, too?"

"Sure. All up and down the west coast, surfers from Canada to Cabo know you as BeeBee."

"Sheesh!" She said.

"Sheesh." Repeated Manny.

"*Sheesh!*" Shouted the rest of the boys.

Mitch sat in the sand to collect himself without his friends knowing he was sick. "Paco, how about those boards?"

Eight young Mexican boys swiveled their collective heads towards Manny's father. Hopeful. Expectant. Eager.

Paco waved for them to follow. With a raucous cheer, the older man led all eight boys back to the locked shed and their boards.

Sandy sat in the sand next to Mitch. "They're lovely, Mitch."

"My surfing animal friends are . . . *lovely*?"

"Yes. Especially Felipe. He's all you said about him. Small, but intense with a gleam in his eyes."

"He's all that and more. A very special kid. I'm gonna miss him. *All* of them."

Sandy's head dropped.

"What?" Mitch asked.

She lifted her head. Tears ran down both cheeks. "*They* will miss you more."

Then it hit him. Mitch had been so consumed with the smell of the surf, the boys and the excitement, he forgot this trip was more than likely his surfing swan song. At least, so it would be for the boys. Would they be able to understand? Mitch gone. Forever. Would Mondo and the others continue to come down and help the boys? Maybe not. After all, Mitch was the special ed teacher. He held the magic key to open their hearts and minds to the treasures surfing offered them. Mitch shed light into their tiny, dark worlds.

"Crap!" Mitch said. "I hadn't given any thought how to tell these guys I will never be back."

"Don't."

"Can't."

"Then don't." She said.

"Okay. But help me get through this trip looking as normal as possible. I feel awful."

"You should." She said.

"Thanks."

"Mitch," She said, "Most people who have what you have are in their jammies in front of the five o'clock news sipping ice water and tossing back meds. You really *should* feel like shit."

"Well, I do."

"You look like shit, too."

"*Sandy!* I can't even *take* a shit."

She howled. Mitch scowled, then broke up until it hurt too much.

Fifteen

One by one, the boys returned, each with a battered and dated surfboard tucked under one arm. Like soldiers, they lined up in the dunes between Mitch and the ocean. Sandy giggled some. Mitch smiled.

"We go?" Renaldo said.

Mitch nodded. Struggled to stand.

"What are *you* doing?" Sandy said in a whisper.

Still smiling, Mitch leaned over to her, "Goin' surfin'."

"Mitch, no."

"Mitch, yes." He said, not looking at her. He was off with the boys. Paco and Sandy stood side by side watching the group kick up sand towards the water.

"Mitch no look good." Paco said.

"Yes. Mitch no look good." Sandy mumbled. She stared. The *boys* no longer five and six, some were in their twenties. All were young men.

Normally, Mitch took one boy at a time out beyond the breakers. They would sit and roll with the waves. Chat some, laugh a lot. Then Mitch would help them pick a wave and in they'd come.

Not today.

Today all eight boys paddled out with Mitch. Well beyond the breakers. Mitch had them form a loose circle sitting on their boards. And they chatted. Laughed.

"What's he do out there?" Sandy asked Paco.

The older man grinned. "Teach."

"Teach what?"

"Your language. Numbers. Surfing." Paco choked up a little. "Mitch teach Paco your language, English."

She smiled. "Not surprised."

"But surfing is the language of Mister Mitch." Paco said. "When Mitch talk surfing, boys learn. Understand."

Helps me to understand some things, too. Sandy thought.

"I thought he took them out one at a time." She said.

"Yes. Today different."

Yes, Paco, it sure is.

"Try to move your boards around into a circle around me." Mitch tried to yell to the boys.

"Not hear Mister Mitch." Jose said.

Mitch motioned for them to move closer.

They did.

They did whatever Mitch asked of them.

He was Mitch. *Mister Mitch.*

Mitch sat in he center, eying each eager face. "Do you remember?"

"Yes." They echoed.

"Jose, tell us when the first wave starts a new set."

They waited. Then Jose barked.

"Count them out." Mitch said.

He did.

"Renaldo, how many gulls in that group." Mitch pointed to a small flock of seagulls holding steady in the gusting wind above the shore.

"Seven."

"Very good."

"If we start out as usual, which one of you would be first?" Mitch asked.

All eight shouted, "Alonzo!" As always, Alonzo, thrilled, turned his board.

"Hold it, Beach Boy!" Mitch tried to shout. He choked. Held his stomach.

Alonzo stopped.

"Today we will reverse the alphabetical order." Mitch said. "We'll do it in reverse."

Blank looks.

"Reverse. Go backwards."

Semi-blank looks.

Mitch thought, "Last goes first."

Faces lit up in deep thought.

Finally, Renaldo shouted, "Me!"

"Are you sure?" Mitch asked.

More thought. One boy was seen writing with a finger on his wet hand. Then Manny shouted. "*Raul!*"

Mitch only nodded. His chest hurt. Throat throbbed. Head spun.

Raul turned and led the group into a long line waiting for the right wave. Mitch stayed back regrouping. He was proud of his boys. Shivered at the thought of never seeing them again. Worse, them never seeing him again. He knew they'd be crushed.

Then he pondered what Sandy had told him about Heaven. She said he'd be welcome.

Mitch wondered if he'd make it.

Raul caught a good wave. He looked solid as if he'd been surfing every day since Mitch and his buddies left. Even attempted toes on the nose. Did fine for three seconds, then wiped out. He popped up screaming with joy.

This was what it was all about. At the same time, both Sandy and Mitch smiled the same thought.

Mitch helped the other boys figure out who was next in his reverse order lesson. Alonzo was last. He was the oldest of the boys at twenty-eight. Physically, Alonzo had a gymnast's build.

Mentally, he was a fast learner, smart. Emotionally, a powder keg. Until Mitch and surfing entered his life.

"Waves are big today, Mister Mitch." Alonzo said, patiently watching the set as it heaved beneath him.

"Yep." Mitch said, also watching for one he didn't want Alonzo to miss.

It came.

Alonzo was talking. Might have missed it, but Mitch pointed to the fourth wave in the set.

"Try number . . ." Mitch waited for Alonzo to finish his sentence.

Alonzo counted. Grinned. "Number four."

"Yes."

The strong boy paddled into position and was gone. It was a bigger than usual wave. Great shape. Alonzo attacked the lip, almost lost it, then re-entered the wave. He disappeared from Mitch's view for several seconds, then appeared farther down the beach. Near the end he negotiated a perfect prone out. Then sat up on his board and waved to Mitch. The others on the beach cheered. It had been a good ride.

Mitch's turn.

He wasn't sure he had it in him.

A sudden throbbing behind his breastbone caused him to shudder head to toe. He convulsed, threw up with his back to the beach.

"God, if you're listening . . . okay, why should you, right? Well, for Sandy's sake, give me one good wave. *Please!*"

None came.

Mitch watched set after set. Shook his head. Caught a modest wave and surfed straight in with nothing fancy. Nevertheless, the boys screamed their enthusiasm. Begged for more when Mitch stood up in the shallow water.

"Okay, one at a time. But let's take a break." Mitch said. He was white-sand pale.

"Sit, *Mister Mitch!*" Sandy said with as much enthusiasm as she could muster. "What the hell were you thinking?"

"Wasn't." Mitch replied.

"Duh."

Paco handed Mitch a broken coffee mug with water in it. Mitch looked down into the clear fluid. Sand sat at the bottom. He smiled. He couldn't have asked for more.

He held it down. Struggled, but it stayed down.

By dinner, the sun down, cooler air swept in off the ocean. It was typical September weather. Paco, a single father, with the help of Jose and Renaldo's mothers, prepared a feast for Mitch's and Sandy's arrival. And a grand day of surfing. The boys' spirits were high. They babbled like busy chipmunks storing their winter food. Everyone was excited.

"How long will you stay, Mister Mitch?" Asked Renaldo's mother.

Mitch was fighting to keep his warm water down. Sandy jumped in.

"Not long. Mitch and I have business to attend to back in the states. We hope to stay a few days, then return."

The woman, a round, happy sort, leaned over to Sandy. "Him no look good."

Sandy glanced around to see no one was too near, "Him sick."

Sixteen

Finding no comfort in the VW bus, Mitch kissed Sandy sometime during the night. Said he had to pee and slid out the side door, closing it behind him. Around the small, cold fire from the evening before, three boys slept in the sand behind the bus.

Mitch picked up his board and stumbled through the dark to the beach.

Felipe!

Asleep in his lean-to. Mitch settled in nearby. Stretched out flat on his back, his head on his board. He swiveled his butt back and forth until he settled into a sand-bed that fit him perfectly. Above, stars salted the black sky. At his feet, Felipe. A small, young man Mitch had grown to love and admire. He loved them all. Closed his eyes to picture each one. Alonzo on his board. Porfirio riding a crest. Raul negotiating a handstand before wiping out. Each boy special.

"Mister Mitch?" Felipe said.

Mitch opened his eyes. He'd been sleeping. First light had crept over the distant hills to the east. Too dark to surf.

"We surf?"

"Sure." Mitch said with no further thought. He felt good. Stronger than he had in days. Swallowing was still difficult, but not impossible.

"Waves big." Felipe said, standing with his board.

"Yep." Glancing west towards No-Name Island.

Wow! Yes, indeed, they are, Felipe.

Together, Mitch and Felipe paddled out beyond the bigger than usual breakers. Beyond where they normally stopped for a brief lesson. And farther still. They paddled. No talk, just paddle. Mitch in the lead. Felipe easily kept up just off Mitch's right shoulder. It was quiet once they were far from the breakers. Swells turned them side to side, but they continued to paddle.

"Island!" Felipe shouted.

Mitch only nodded. He still felt good. Strong. Confused by it, but not willing to look a gift horse in the mouth. Or Sandy's God, for that matter.

They rolled onto the small beach at No-Name Island. Though against the incoming surf and current, they were both strong. The small beach was inviting, but they could not stay. Mitch knew Sandy worried.

They had little difficulty paddling back. Neither was tired.

"How was that?" Mitch asked his beaming partner.

"Good, Mister Mitch." Nothing in Felipe's life was better than surfing alone with Mitch.

Behind them, the morning sun lit up the top of the rocky island. It slowly crept down the side through kelp, crags and seagull droppings until swallowing the two men paddling on their boards towards the beach.

Felipe sat up on his board close to his hero. His was not of a mind to question, just take what life handed out. And this was a moment he'd lived for.

"We surf?"

"Yep. With this wind and the breakers we saw coming out, we could catch a good one going back."

"Mitch okay?" Came a haunting question Mitch had hoped none of the boys would ask.

"Nope." Mitch couldn't, wouldn't lie to his buddy.

"Sick bad?"

"Yep."

"Felipe help Mitch?"

"You already have, my friend. Already have."

Felipe seemed satisfied with that answer. "We go back?"

"Let's do it."

Padding with the tide was easier. They made good time returning to their lesson spot behind the breakers.

"Crap!" Mitch said.

Felipe looked where Mitch was looking. Some twenty people had gathered on the beach by Felipe's campsite. Closer to the water, BeeBee stood, looking none too happy. Waving. Shouting something inaudible. Mitch was glad he couldn't understand what she was saying. Knew it wasn't what he wanted to hear.

"Okay, Felipe. You wait for your wave. They're good today. The best I've ever seen here. What a surfer calls, *big surf.* Look for a Bombora. A big ass wave bigger than all the others. Be patient. Wait for it."

He did.

Set after set rolled by. Many good waves that normally Mitch would have sent Felipe in on. But not today.

They waited.

With wind shifts, Mitch could make out Sandy's voice. Something about getting back to shore. Mitch didn't look towards the beach.

"Mitch?"

"Yeah."

"That Bombora?" Felipe said, pointing.

"Oh, man, is it ever." Mitch hummed. "It's awesome. Angle to your left, then catch it going to your right. It's the biggest wave you've ever surfed."

Even has a barrel to it. But it may be too small to get into. Thought Mitch.

As he wondered about the tube, the wave grew exponentially. Suddenly there was a tunnel big enough to surf a Mack truck through.

Felipe caught the curl, spun to his right and disappeared over the crest. The wave broke and kept breaking. Felipe was out of sight. Locked in. Then, some three hundred yards down the beach, the small boy popped out of the last of the barrel and, with hands held high, he pulled out. Dropped down to his butt on his board. Waved back at Mitch.

With an approving smile, Mitch simply shook his head in proud approval. Then waited for the next Bombora.

It never came. He caught a good wave, made a good run.

Until he stood in front of Sandy. Her arms folded. Neck crimson.

Luckily for Mitch, Felipe and all the other boys immediately gathered around him, cheering and happy.

Mitch locked eyes with the woman of his dreams. Shrugged. Sandy shrugged back, mouthed *I love you* and seemed to let it go.

Later, after each boy had taken a turn surfing the unusually large surf, Mitch and Sandy sat in the sun high atop a dune. One of the mothers brought them each a cup of very dark coffee. Sandy sipped in silence. Mitch pretended to drink his.

He waited for Sandy to unload on him.

Sandy mulled what to unload.

Finally, "Mitch, that was crazy."

"Yep."

"But I get it."

He smiled. Not sure *what* she got, but she hadn't unloaded on him.

"Good, I guess."

"Paco told me that before you, Mondo, and the others started coming down here, these people spoke no English."

He nodded. Held the pain in his chest.

"He said they *were* happy."

Mitch turned to her expecting something bad. *"Were?"*

"Yeah." She said. With a disarming glow, she ran her eyes over his face. Ran a hand across his bearded cheek. "He *thought* they were happy. He and the others had no idea what true happiness was until you and your buddies showed up. Not just to surf, but . . ." She lost it.

"What?"

Through tears, "Mitch, these people love you. Every little bit of your soggy, saltwater body. You embraced them and their boys, not the surf and sun like so many others before you. They have been so enriched by you and your friends. If you keel over right now, you've left a legacy no one will ever be able to measure."

"Hmm." He said. Not sure he got it. "It's been fun."

"But that *stunt* today!"

Stunt? He thought.

"You might have had some sort of seizure out there and drowned."

"I had Felipe with me." He kidded.

She looked at him and shook her head. *He doesn't get it.*

"I think we need to get back to San Diego for your treatment." She announced. Not mad, just matter of fact.

He hadn't caught *his* Bombora. "One more day."

"Why? You've accomplished what we came for."

"Not yet."

"What then?" She asked.

Light rain began dropping. The wind had brought in a passing storm.

"I need me a Bombora."

"A what?"

"Bombora. A wave like Felipe caught. It's Australian for a big ass wave out of the norm."

"Like you."

"Huh?"

"Big ass out of the norm."

His laugh was shortened by a sharp pain above the stomach. He threw up what little water he'd taken in.

"One more day, Bombora or no Bombora." She scowled.

He nodded.

Mitch didn't get his Bombora. He didn't even get his next day on the beach.

What he did get was a non-stop drive back to San Diego and straight to Rodin's office.

Seventeen

"It's metastasized to his liver and his stomach." Rodin said to Sandy. Mitch slumped next to her.

"Did our little expedition cause that?" Sandy said, eying Mitch.

"Doubt it." Scanlon said. "It's just the nature of stage four esophageal cancer to spread like this if we don't get to it early enough."

"What now?"

"Palliative therapy." Rodin said, like the couple should know what it was.

They stared blank at the doctors.

"I'll be frank. Surgery is *not* an option. Palliative therapy is chemotherapy or radiation to reduce the symptoms. There is no cure. All we can do is . . ."

"Make me feel as comfortable as possible." Mitch mumbled.

"Yes."

"What can we expect now?"

"Weight loss. Your swallowing could get worse, even with the stent." Scanlon said.

"Pneumonia." Rodin added. "We must not get pneumonia."

"We?" Mitch said.

"Sorry." Rodin said.

There was a long, pregnant pause before Mitch choked, then spoke. "Okay, I'm going to die. When?"

Scanlon started to speak, but Rodin cut him off. "Mitch, there is no accurate assessment of how long you have left. To be honest, you have been on borrowed time since the day we diagnosed it."

Sandy started to cry.

Mitch put an arm around her. "So, which is it? Chemo or radiation?"

"Radiation." Scanlon said. Rodin nodded.

"Then let's get to it." Mitch said.

Sixteen days later, hundreds of Mitch's best friends gathered around the end of a long finger of water off San Diego Harbor. Sandy and their children. Mondo, Pounder, Stringer and Dog. Surfers from as far as Vancouver, Canada and Brisbane, Australia. Every member of every team or club Mitch was involved in.

Five small boats were launched from a pier at the end of the inlet. One was for his four surfing buddies. One for Sandy and her three adult children. They made a circle much like Mitch would circle the Ejido Chapala boys beyond the breakers off the coast of Baja.

One by one, they held high a portion of Mitch's ashes, then cast them into the water.

Sandy was last.

She clutched the small wooden box to her chest. Her shoulders shuddered.

Then abruptly, she unfolded and swung her arm across the sky. The ashes flew from the small box in a curved line above Sandy's head. Lingered above her as if to say goodbye, then dissipated in all directions.

"Go, Mitch. *You can make it!*" Sandy hushed to herself.

Her son sat at the other end of the small boat. "Make *what*, Mom?"

"Heaven." She said, sniffling openly. "Your father was worried he'd go to Hell."

Slowly, each boat returned to the pier. They all gathered at the end, staring at the calm waters where Mitch now rested in peace.

Most of him.

At home, Sandy and Dog had prepared eight match boxes, one for each boy. Each sealed with some of Mitch's ashes. In three days, Sandy and the four surfers were traveling to Ejido Chapala for a similar ceremony with Paco and the boys.

Eighteen

As if Mitch was with them, Sandy and the surfers followed their usual routine driving to visit the boys on the beach in Baja.

Dog, now Sandy riding shotgun, drove one bus with all the surfboards. Mondo, Pounder, Stringer and supplies in the other. An overnight stay in Ensenada and by dinner the next day they arrived in the small village of Ejido Chapala.

Late as it was in the year, no one was surprised a storm was moving in off the coast. Actually, the four men were excited about the waves that the wind and rain usually pushed towards the shore.

As the two buses bounced and splashed through muddy puddles en route to where they usually camped on the beach, Dog couldn't help thinking about Mitch.

"Mitch would have loved this." He said. "This was *his* kind of weather. Warm with storm warnings. The waves can be spectacular."

Sandy, holding on for dear life as the bus careened from side to side, nodded she knew. "Can't tell you how many mornings over the years I woke up during a storm to an empty bed. Mitch would be down at Pacific Beach before anyone else. *Shootin' the pier* he'd say when he finally got home."

"Crazy thing to do." Dog said, fighting the steering wheel.

"Do you shoot the pier?"

"Hell, yes. We all do."

She laughed. "Figures."

"What?"

"You're all crazy."

"True."

Minutes later, Dog pulled into a clearing behind a stand of trees along the beach. Stringer, not far behind, eased up along side. Both drivers pinched the latch to slide their respective driver's windows open.

Stringer yelled over the wind. "Big storm. Maybe we should backtrack to Ejido Chapala and take a room in the hotel."

"Why?" Dog asked.

Stringer raised his eyebrows and nodded towards Sandy, leaning from the front passenger seat to hear the conversation.

Dog turned to Sandy.

She to him. "Would Mitch go to a hotel because of a storm?"

Dog shook his head. "Not hardly." He turned back to Stringer. "We stay here as always."

Abruptly, Paco appeared between the two buses, smiling. His son, Manuel, was with him. "You made it." He yelled, holding tight to his battered work hat. "I am glad, but sorry for, you know."

Sandy nodded. Paco knew about Mitch, but none of the boys knew.

"Hi Paco. Hi Manny. Yeah. And we have Mitch's wife with us. You've already met Sandy, right?"

Paco peered at her. "Yes. We meet. You still as pretty as Mitch say."

She blushed a little. "And you are as smooth as he said."

Everyone laughed except Manny who didn't get it. He was looking for Mitch.

Sandy got out of the bus. The wind whipped her long hair. It wasn't raining at the moment. She came to Manny. She knew Down syndrome when she saw it. She put out a hand for him to shake. "Hi, Manny."

Manny ran past the extended hand and gave Sandy a big hug. She him. Paco smiled with a shake of his head. Then, "Will you be camping here as usual?"

"Yep."

"You will get very wet."

"Yep."

"Can I get you anything?"

"Manny's all we need for now." Dog said.

The camp was nestled in and amongst the thick trees. They provided some shelter from the rain and wind. Dog set up a latrine for the men and gave Sandy the portable toilet. Told her about a nook at the other end of the trees. She left for the nook.

"How's she doing?" Pounder asked Dog.

"Seems fine. We talked all the way down. She cried from time to time, but basically she seems at peace with the whole thing."

"This storm should bring us serious ground swells. Mitch would have loved this."

There was a long pause as all four men suddenly became lost in memories of Mitch and all the things he loved.

And would miss.

"I sure miss him." Mondo said, his voice cracking.

"Yeah. Me, too." Said Dog.

"We all do." Sandy said, coming in from the beach side of the trees. "There's a lean-to and fire pit down by the beach."

"Belongs to Felipe. It's where he'd stay when we were here."

"You guys slept here and Felipe down there?" She said.

"Yep. Felipe's quite the independent kid."

"Speaking of *kids*." Sandy said. "These boys aren't boys anymore, are they?"

"No. They are all, physically, young men." Dog said.

"Probably twenty to twenty-eight."

"And you still refer to them as boys." Sandy said.

"Yes. Most are still stuck in neutral as far as aging mentally. But don't underestimate any of them. They are crafty, smart and strong."

"And not necessarily in that order."

Paco arrived, Manny not with him. "I take Manny home. None of the boys know about Mister Mitch. I not have the heart to tell them."

Sandy put an arm around the smaller man. "It's okay, Paco. You shouldn't have to tell them. We can do it."

I think.

"Felipe will be hard to tell." Paco said.

Pounder nodded. Said to Sandy, "Felipe and Mitch were especially close. Beyond the surfing."

Felipe was the first to arrive, immediately asking for Mitch. His surfboard wobbled in the wind on his shoulder. He stood it beside him.

"You look like you're ready to hit the surf, Felipe." Dog said.

"No. Felipe never surf after dark." He said. "Where Mister Mitch?"

"Felipe, sit down by the fire. We'll wait for the others to arrive."

Immediately wary, Felipe grabbed his board, slid off into the shadows. Set his board down flat on the ground and sat on it. The fire's flame danced and flickered shadows across his face. Reflected in his dark brown eyes. Soon the others arrived. Each with his board. Paco and Manny were the last of the group. They all sat around the blazing bonfire.

Felipe refused to move in to join them. He was suspicious. He stood. "Where is Mister Mitch?"

Sandy rose to her feet. She was on the opposite side of the fire from Felipe. She studied the slope of his shoulders, the teary glisten in his eyes. His head cocked to one side.

He knows. She thought. *How could he know?*

"For those of you who don't know, I'm Sandy. Missus Mitch."

Mondo chuckled. The other men grinned.

The boys and Paco remained stoic. Emotionless.

"Mister Mitch is not here." She said. "But he asked me to give you something."

She lifted her backpack and removed the eight tightly sealed matchboxes with a tablespoon of Mitch's ashes in each. She slowly walked around the fire handing one to each boy. As each boy took it, she touched his head affectionately, but said nothing. Felipe was the last. He was reluctant to reach out, but finally took the small, taped box.

Sandy returned to face them.

"When he be here?" Renaldo shouted.

Jose said the same.

Porfirio stood. Paced. Mumbled many things no one could understand. He turned away from the fire and wrung his hands.

"He's here now." Sandy said, choking on her words. "You have him in your hands."

A gust of wind tossed embers across the sand. A few rain drops slashed sideways into the campers.

Felipe stood, stared at the box in his small palm as if it were a dead tarantula. He rose and approached the fire. From across the fire pit, through the rising warm air and smoke, he met Sandy's eyes. Said nothing.

Sandy looked around, then at Felipe. "Mitch won't be surfing on this trip." Her voice trembled. They all heard it.

"*When!*" Shouted Felipe.

"I'm so sorry, but . . ."

As if he *had* read her thoughts, Felipe screamed a loud *No!* Yanked up his board and ran off into the dark. Two others followed. The remaining five boys didn't understand yet.

In a soft voice, the oldest of the boys, Alonzo, repeated the question. "When?"

"Never." Yelled Mondo.

Paco gripped his son around the shoulders. All understood but Jose, who asked. "He never surf with boys again?"

"No." Sandy said. "Mister Mitch was very sick."

"He die?"

"Yes."

"Why?"

"Very sick."

"Sad."

"Y-yes, it is." Sandy was struggling.

As if the music had stopped, the punch bowl drained and the lights dimmed, each boy slowly stood. Each embraced his surfboard as he might embrace Mitch after a good run. Each stared aimlessly at the fire, then at Sandy, then at the matchbox, then peeled out of the glow into the numbing black that surrounded them.

Each meandered alone into the dark solitude the wind and dunes can provide a broken heart.

Only Sandy and her four friends remained around the fire. Its flames roiling sideways in the wind. Hissing when the rain landed on coals.

"Not how I wanted that to go." Sandy said.

"How else could it go?" Pounder said.

"Better."

"For who?"

Sandy had to think about that. There was no way to tell them and make it *better*. Mitch was gone. Their surfer god, Mister Mitch, would no longer be coming to see them. The big Kahuna, who helped them understand things others would never take the time to teach them. Numbers. The difference between a glassy ocean and a gnarly ocean. How to be patient for the right wave. When to say thank you. Why it's not smart to night surf or go alone to No-Name Island. And when to yell, Kowabunga.

Sandy turned to the four men, each pondering his own Mitch thoughts. "What are your intentions?"

"About?"

"These young men. They so look up to you guys."

"They looked up to Mitch. He knew how to reach them. How to teach in a way they got it. Hell, he could teach them anything, and they'd get it. He was terrific with them."

Yes, he was.

"So, then, you guys are no longer going to come down here?"

They looked back and forth amongst themselves. "Not sure." Stringer said, his head bowed.

"It wouldn't be the same without Mitch." Mondo said.

"What he was to these boys, he was no less to us." Pounder added. "He was our best friend."

Mine, too. Sandy thought.

"You can't quit these boys. Mitch wouldn't." She said.

"I'm no Mitch." Dog said. "I've never been sure just how to behave around, you know, kids with issues."

"But you kept coming down." Sandy argued.

"We had Mitch." Pounder said.

"Yeah, the boys spent most of their time with Mister Mitch." Mondo said. "We just surfed and helped when he needed us."

Sandy needed to think. She yawned.

Then two of the men yawned. "Been a long day." Dog said. "I'm turnin' in."

"Can we discuss this further in the morning?" Sandy continued.

Each nodded or mumbled something in the affirmative.

But they never would.

Nineteen

The snap of a branch breaking was louder than the surf beyond the trees. That in itself got Sandy's attention.

The wind had continued its endless roar. No rain.

Sandy woke with a start. She'd fallen asleep curled up by the fire. Someone had covered her with a blanket, but it had blown off, tangled about at her feet. She was wet from an earlier misty rain. She was not cold.

Another snapped of a branch and a thud. Sounded like someone had tripped and fallen. Someone or some *thing* was plodding along through the trees towards them in the dark.

"Missus Mitch! Dog! Mondo!"

Paco's shadowy form hobbled out of the trees into the cleared campsite.

"Over here, Paco." Sandy said. She tried to stand. A gust of wind pushed her almost into the cold fire pit.

Dog and Stringer slid out from under one bus. Mondo jumped from his bus. Pounder was peeing in the trees.

"T-the boys." Paco gasped. He was out of breath.

"What? They alright?"

"All gone. Take boards."

"Shit!" Sandy said to everyone's surprise. She turned in the direction of the ocean. Trees blocked her view.

"Listen." Dog hushed.

A young man's voice bounced in and out of the gusting wind and thunderous waves. Sandy led them at a run around the stand of trees. Though still dark, the first hint of morning's light in the east helped them see the foamy surf and distant horizon.

And eight young men standing in a row, side by side next to their tall surfboards.

Each as if at attention. The boards wobbled in the wind.

Each clutched a small matchbox in his hand.

Abruptly, Felipe moved out in front of the others. Stared at the billowing waves, then turned and stood in front facing the other seven. He spoke in Spanish.

Dog whispered to Sandy. "This was how Mitch got them started every morning. Lined them up so they could listen to his instructions for the day."

"In the dark like this?" She asked.

"No. This is a little unusual." Dog said. He started to move forward towards the boys, but Sandy put an arm out to stop him.

"Let's see what they do." She said.

The raging waves pounded the beach. Wind tossed foam almost into the trees. Now, slashing raindrops pelted the sand around them.

Sandy, Paco and the four surfers eased around the trees, then sat huddled against the gale to watch. Occasionally Felipe's voice could be heard. Paco interpreted.

"He say they follow Mister Mitch."

Sandy panicked. "Follow? Mitch is dead!"

Paco leaned to her. "No! Not follow to be dead. Follow *lessons.*"

"Thank God." She mumbled.

Yes. Thank you, Father.

The rain picked up. The wind blew it sideways.

Felipe continued to speak.

"Numbers something." Paco relayed.

Then, one after the other, the boys counted off, one through eight. Felipe turned and entered the pounding surf. Raul followed.

Then Manny. And so on until Alonzo brought up the rear. All of them struggled against the waves and wind.

"Maybe we should stop them. It's damn rough out there." Stringer said.

"Not yet." Sandy said.

"Easy for you to say, BeeBee." Mondo laughed. She laughed, too. Sandy surfed, but was not a surfer.

One by one, the boys finally paddled through the crashing waves until each made it out far enough behind the breakers for them to circle their boards. It was difficult against the wind and swells. Today, their usual gathering place had to be farther out due to the storm. In the east, a morning sun was fighting the heavy, black clouds. It was getting light enough to see the boys fighting to maintain their circle.

Felipe sat on his board in the middle. Arms animated.

"I can't hear him." Pounder yelled, shielding his eyes from the rain.

"Lesson." Paco shouted.

Felipe had peeled off from the end of the line the boys had formed in the sand. He glanced back at the others, each riveted to the ocean. Waves like they'd never seen before.

He turned back around to them. Held his matchbox high in the air. "We go. Say goodbye to Mister Mitch. *Count!*"

The boys stiffened as if waiting for military orders. One or more sobbed.

Felipe yelled "One!"

Raul barked number two. Finally, Alonzo yelled number eight and one at a time they entered the pounding surf. Felipe was at first tossed backwards. Raul caught him. None of them had ever seen an ocean like this.

Felipe paddled with all his strength. Once clear of the breakers, he looked back. Behind him each boy was paddling for all he was worth until they met behind the breakwater.

"Make a circle." Felipe yelled.

It wasn't easy, but they managed to circle their boards tightly around Felipe. One at a time he made eye contact with each of the young surfers. Then, "We are how many?"

Together they shouted, "*Eight!*"

"Cut in half."

"*Four!*" They yelled back at him.

"Add two."

"*Six!*"

"If I surf in, how many behind in water?"

"*Seven!*"

Felipe paused, tired of the lesson. Again, he held up the small box containing his best friend in all the world. He voice cracked. "*Who will miss Mister Mitch?*"

No one answered.

Jose could no longer contain himself and broke into uncontrolled sobs. Then Porfirio and Manny. Felipe said nothing. He, too, wanted to cry, but knew Mitch would want him to be strong for the others.

"Open the box."

Fighting the wind, the turbulent swells and their emotions, each boy ripped off the end of the sealed matchbox.

What happened next was never explained to the adults huddling on shore. And for that matter, none of the boys was equipped to explain it. Felipe instructed them all to pour Mitch's ashes at one time in the same place. He figured that might bring Mitch back if they consolidated all the pieces.

The circling boys opened a gap for Felipe to slide into. They tightened the circle so all their boards met, leaving a three foot circle in the center. When he gave the signal, each boy reached out and poured the gray ashes into the center of the circle.

At that moment, the sea stopped its roll.

The wind ceased.

The rain surrounded them, but did not fall upon them.

Then a voice they knew all too well came out of the water around them. It was clear and deep. It called out to each boy by his first name.

Then, "I love you. Tell Sandy I *made* it. It will please her."

Wide-eyed and startled, the boys looked back and forth between themselves. Some cried. Some looked into the water. Some smiled.

Manny laughed."Mister Mitch?"

There was no doubt.

Felipe looked renewed. He sat up tall on his surfboard. Looked with clear understanding at each of his surfing buddies.

"Mister Mitch surfing with us back to beach."

Some understood. Others, not so much. Regardless, each boy was eager to catch a big one.

"We surf back." Felipe said. "One at a time so Mister Mitch can watch. Alonzo go first."

As was the custom, the boys broke up the circle and lined up behind the breakers. Alonzo pulled out. The usual waves that came in at this particular location were two waves converging around No-Name Island. It was why Mitch and his friends liked it. The contours of the sand below and around No-Name Island created some of the best point breaks any of them had ever seen. They were steady and consistently good for surfing. Today was no different, except the swells were huge. Most eight to ten feet high compared to the usual four to six.

Most impressive on this day was the long, seemingly endless breaks that ran for hundreds of yards.

"Mitch miss good waves." Manny said.

"Maybe not." Felipe said.

Alonzo didn't wait long. The froth and wind pushed against him as he waited for the wave he wanted. Then he began his paddle. Gained speed. The wave broke and he began his takeoff. For the boys behind him, Alonzo quickly disappeared.

The men and lady on the beach cheered.

Sandy gasped when Alonzo stood up on his board. She'd seen it a million times, but there was no Mitch out there to help.

"He's caught a pounder." Pounder said.

"Cute, Big Guy." Dog said with a laugh.

They all watched as Alonzo shot the curl, then pulled out and coasted into the shore. He stood, picked up his board and waved for Carlos to begin.

"Carlos." Mondo said. He liked Carlos. An extra big kid like himself, Mondo had taught Carlos a few things Mitch hadn't shown the other boys.

Carlos rode the tube until near the end, then he walked ahead on his board and hung his toes over the front.

"*Damn!*" Exclaimed Stringer. "Where'd he learn that?"

Mondo beamed.

One boy after another took his individual turn. Mitch taught them to wait for each to finish so each could learn from the other. As well as admire how their friends were surfing. When Raul stood in the shallow water, he waved for Felipe to begin.

Felipe sat on his board watching the waves.

Waiting for the right one.

Twenty

"He's been waiting a long time." Sandy said. "Looked to me there were plenty of good ones."

"Felipe's the best of them." Stringer said. "No doubt he wants to catch a really big one."

"*Yipes!*" Yelled Dog. "Like *that* one." He pointed.

All looked.

"*Shit!*"

"What do you think? Fifteen?"

"Maybe twenty."

"What are you guys talking about?" Sandy asked.

"Feet high." Pounder said. "We loved this spot because we got steady six foot swells."

"Yeah. Good enough for surfing. Great for teaching."

"So, is a fifteen or twenty too big?" Sandy said as a wall of water began to gather in the distance behind Felipe.

"Could be." Dog whispered into the wind.

Felipe's heart pounded as the mountain of water approached. *Bombora!* He thought.

He started to paddle. Gained momentum. The swell lifted him higher than he'd ever been, then began to break. Felipe started his takeoff. His heart skipped a beat. The salt spray, wind and roar of the waves too much to ignore.

Then something inexplicable.

The same voice spoke to him in his mind. "Kowabunga, Dude."

Felipe smiled and paddled hard to catch the wave.

From the beach, Sandy and the others watched Felipe study the oncoming monster wave.

"He's gonna catch it." Mondo said.

Then Felipe turned to paddle with the wave.

A mondo wave.

"Look at that." Pounder said.

"Damn!"

"That one will have a really long barrel."

"Outrageous."

"Maybe twenty-five."

"Kowabunga."

Several of the boys studied the swell approaching Felipe. They echoed *kowabunga*. Screamed with joy when Felipe stood up on his board.

Then he was on the peak and over the crest and down the wall of the wave.

And into the tube.

His balance was perfect. He crouched to hold the rail of his board with his left hand. Dropped to one knee. Ran his right hand along the back wall of the tube. Screamed with delight as he raced along between the falling lip and the open wall.

"Amazing." Dog said.

"Damned amazing." Pounder said.

"Wish that was me." Dog scowled.

Sandy moved forward, squinting. "Guys, I've seen Mitch do that a million times. I have never seen anyone else surf like that."

All eyes focused hard on Felipe.

"Like Mitch is with him" Stringer mumbled.

"Does" Mondo said. "Fantastic technique."

To their collective amazement, Felipe rode up and down the wall of the tube.

"You guys seein' this?"

"Looks a helluva lot like Mitch."

"Sure does. Felipe's been a good student."

"Like you said, it looks more like Mitch than Felipe." Sandy said sarcastically to Mondo.

"No way." Mondo laughed.

Sandy laughed too.

Felipe finished far down the beach. He grabbed his board and splashed up to the beach and started running for the group.

They all rushed to greet him. Pound his back. Congratulate him. Sandy hugged him. Mondo squeezed him. Paco simply shook his head in amazement.

Felipe nodded to the other boys who then formed a circle around Sandy.

"What?" She said with a smile, circling to each happy face.

"We put Mitch into the sea." Manny said.

"His ashes." Sandy said.

"Yes." Porfirio replied.

"I'm glad. Thank you. Mitch loved each of you so much." Sandy said, her eyes tearing up.

"Mitch tell us he love us." Jose said.

"Each of us." Raul said, excited.

"I know. Yes, he loved you."

"Mitch have message for Missus Mitch." Renaldo smiled.

"What?" Sandy was confused. Wiped away the tears.

Felipe stepped forward in front of Sandy. "Mitch in the sea tell us to tell Sandy he *made* it."

He made it? Sandy thought.

"Oh, my God." Sandy sobbed big heaves. Wrapped her arms around Felipe. Squeezed the boy hard.

"Mister Mitch say you be happy."

"I am, Felipe. I am."

End

14946393R00053

Made in the USA
Charleston, SC
09 October 2012